THE ILIAD

STORIES OF THE TROJAN WARS

HAMLYN

English translation by Karin Sisti

Illustrated by Libico Maraja

First published by Piero Dami Editore under the title
Iliade La Guerra Di Troia
© Copyright 1982 Falcon Books Inc., U.S.A.

This edition published in 1985 by
Hamlyn Publishing,
a division of The Hamlyn Publishing Group Limited,
Bridge House, London Road,
Twickenham, Middlesex, England.

© Copyright 1985, English language edition Hamlyn
Publishing, a division of The Hamlyn Publishing
Group Limited.

ISBN 0 600 31061 2
Printed in Italy

A terrible row breaks out between Achilles and Agamemnon

BOOK I

For nine years war had been raging under the walls of Troy. For nine years Greeks and Trojans had been engaged in a terrible war without one or the other being favoured by a decisive victory. For nine years they had fought and died.

Now was a time of truce. But the Greeks were still dying. They were dying of a strange illness to which there was no known remedy. It was a clear sign of Apollo's wrath. But why such anger?

'Why?' asked Achilles, King of the Myrmidons, the strongest of all the warriors. 'Calchas, our priest and prophet, tell us the reason. Why does the god Apollo persecute us so? How have we offended him?'

Silence fell on the assembly of the Greek princes and Calchas, with a stern face and frowning forehead, replied, 'Apollo wants to punish he who holds as a slave the girl Chryseis, daughter of Chryses – the angered god's chosen priest. Chryses, you will remember, came here to ask for his daughter's release but met with a blunt refusal. For this Apollo strikes us.'

These words were greeted by a general whisper and all turned to Agamemnon, the supreme leader of the Greeks. It was he who held the lovely Chryseis as his slave, it therefore fell to him to placate Apollo's wrath by returning her to her father. But no one dared to speak. No one except Achilles who said, 'King, do what you must. Give up the girl.'

'Give her up?' asked Agamemnon haughtily, 'I, the leader? I can do, yes, but on one condition. In exchange for Chryseis, I want a slave as young and as beautiful as she. And I know just where to find one.'

'Perhaps you are thinking of Briseis, my own slave?' asked the troubled Achilles.

'Precisely,' came the harsh answer, 'and if you do not give her to me I shall take her myself!'

Achilles felt burning anger rise in his chest, and it was with great difficulty that he controlled himself and checked the impulse to reach for his sword. Trembling with rage he said, 'So that is your wish, is it? You want to take away from me

what I have fought for! The Trojans have never done me any harm, they have never offended me in any way, and yet I am fighting against them! And for whom? For you, you coward! I have left my country, I have come here and risked my life because a Trojan, Paris, has abducted Helen your brother's wife! You said the offence done to Menelaus was an offence to the whole of Greece, and we listened to you! We came to Troy and we have fought – and I, harder than anybody else! Is this to be my reward?'

In the frozen silence, Achilles went on, 'Beware Agamemnon, if you take Briseis away from me, I shall no longer fight. I shall sail back to Greece with my men!'

'Go, if you are afraid! We shall go on fighting without you!' Agamemnon cried.

For a moment it seemed that Achilles and Agamemnon were about to leap at each other's throats, but Nestor – the eldest and wisest of the Greeks – spoke up severely. 'Calm down both of you! Can't you see that you are only favouring the Trojans by behaving in this way? Agamemnon, you cannot take Briseis from Achilles and Achilles, you must have more respect for the king!'

These were wise words, but spoken in vain. Achilles contemptuously left the assembly and retired to his camp.

Soon afterwards two of Agamemnon's messengers arrived at his camp to fetch Briseis. Achilles raised no objection. He ordered Patroclus, his dearest and most loyal friend, 'Fetch the girl!'

Pale faced, Achilles watched Briseis as she was led away in tears.

A few days went by and a Greek ship entered the port of Chryse. Odysseus, King of Ithaca, stepped ashore and solemnly returned Chryseis to her father.

'Here is your daughter, Chryses – now ask Apollo to spare the Greeks!'

'I shall do so,' replied the priest. 'Come now, let us carry out the required sacrifices!'

Achilles watches the weeping Briseis as she is led away by Agamemnon's messengers

In the meantime, Achilles was beside himself with anger. His companions had never seen him so distraught. After a long outburst of bitter tears he paced along the shores of the crashing seas, trembling and cursing, and suddenly turned towards the sea and cried out, 'Mother! Mother! You who have brought me into this world – if only for a short while – hear me! They have offended me, they have humiliated me!'

He cried and sobbed again until out of the sea where she lived, rose Thetis, his divine mother, troubled to see her son in distress. She came to him and said, 'My child, why are you weeping?'

'You already know the reason, Mother. I beg of you, help me to seek revenge. You are a goddess, go to Zeus, father of all gods, and ask him to support the Trojans, to grant them victory so that the Greeks may see that without me, they have no hope of winning the war! Oh, Mother, I call upon you to hear me! Please help me!'

Moved, Thetis promised, and flew to Olympus, the sacred mountain where the gods assembled. She begged Zeus to help her avenge Achilles' honour and grief. Zeus, frowning, listened to her. The long war was worrying him and dividing all the gods. At last he answered, 'Thetis, I can refuse you nothing. So be it. The Greeks shall pay dearly for the injury they have inflicted upon your son!'

Looking out to sea, Achilles calls out to Thetis, his mother

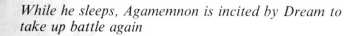

BOOK II

It was night. All the men were asleep, so were all the gods – except Zeus. In his tent, Agamemnon was also asleep when descending swiftly from the heavens, Dream came silently to him and whispered in his ear, 'You sleep Agamemnon, even though you command an army and a fleet! Listen, Zeus has sent me. Through me he speaks. Do not hesitate any longer; gather your troops and move towards Troy. Fight and you shall win. Zeus and the other gods have decided so. Agamemnon, victory is yours. Take it!'

Dream vanished and Agamemnon woke up, deeply impressed. So the gods had decided. He must attack and at once: victory was certain. He got dressed, buckled his sword belt and picked up his sceptre. He never imagined that by sending him Dream and inciting him to battle, Zeus intended to humiliate the Greeks, as he had promised his beloved Thetis. Agamemnon therefore summoned all the princes, and told them about his dream.

'Let us prepare,' he said, 'for the decisive battle. But first, in order to test our soldiers, I shall tell them that the war is over, that we have lost, that we shall never succeed in conquering Troy and that we must abandon our camp. When I have spoken, it will be your turn. Each one of you must speak out and urge his men to remain, exhort them to battle, remind them that the honour of Greece is at stake and that one cannot accept defeat. I am sure', he concluded, 'that this will inspire them to fight ardently and to win. I am certain that tomorrow, Troy shall be ours as I was told by the dream sent to me by Zeus himself.'

So a little while later the whole Greek army was gathered into a huge assembly. When Agamemnon appeared there was a great hush.

'Soldiers,' cried the king, 'nine years have now passed since we arrived on the shores of Troy. Nine years and we have not won. I confess that I have lost all hope of victory. Enough of war! Let us board our ships! Let us resign ourselves to defeat and return to Greece!'

There was a moment of utter silence amongst the soldiers, as though they could not believe what they had heard, then a mighty roar rose from the assembly.

'Home! We are going home!' and they began to run towards the ships. In great confusion, tents were taken down, shelters dismantled, some men were already boarding ships whilst others were launching them out to sea. 'Greece! Greece! Home!'

Odysseus then stepped forward, ran to Agamemnon, snatched the sceptre from his hand and wielding it he addressed the most valiant of the leaders and soldiers.

'Have you gone mad!' he shouted. 'Where are you going? Where are you running to? Don't you understand that he, the powerful king, will punish you if you flee? Stop! Come back! The honour of Greece is at stake!'

At these words many stopped running and suddenly realized they had committed an act of cowardice. Many jumped off the ships and returned to the point of assembly. Among those who were set to go, Thersites – the ugliest and most evil of all the Greeks – shouted and protested louder than anybody else.

'What are you doing? Why are you stopping?' he shouted, running up and down. 'What do you care about Agamemnon and his brother Mene-laus? What do you care about Helen's honour? Home, let's go home, and leave these worthless kings!'

Angered by these words, Odysseus struck at him with the sceptre and knocked him to the ground. The whimpering Thersites tried to pro-tect himself from the blows and the soldiers around him laughed and sniggered and said, 'Odysseus has done some wonderful things in his life, but to shut Thersites' mouth is the most wonderful of all!'

Then Odysseus stood on the platform and addressed the warriors who had gathered around him. 'Greeks, it is true that we have been here for nine years, but it is all the more reason for us to hold on and fight till the end! What purpose will our efforts have served, why will our companions have died if we run away now? We will have failed in our word and disgraced our name! No, Agamemnon, we shall not leave you! Nobody,' he added, 'is thinking of returning home, not before we have taken Troy! Not before we have avenged Helen's honour, and the honour of Greece! But, he concluded threateningly, if any fool wants to leave, let him get to his ship, but let it be known that instead of escaping death he will meet with it instantly.'

From the platform Odysseus tells the soldiers to fight on to victory

*The two entire armies on the battlefield, ready to
confront each other*

In the silence, Agamemnon stepped forward.
'In the name of Greece, my friends, let us then
prepare for the decisive battle! Yes, victory is
ours! Eat now, then sharpen all swords and
spears, and let each man join his rank, his
companions and his prince. We shall attack and
we shall not stop fighting until we are inside
Troy!'

A great cheer acclaimed these words, and a
few hours later the Greeks moved in battle order
towards the city. Those who were able to, had
made offerings to the gods and prayed that they
might be saved from death. But they were all
determined to fight and put an end to the war
which had lasted too long. In a clatter of iron, the
Greek army marched to battle, across the vast
green plain which lay before Troy, and where ran
the rivers Simoenta and Scamander (which the
gods also called Xanthus).

Meanwhile in Troy, a conference was taking
place. The Trojans had gathered around their
wise old King Priam and were discussing the war
and what could be done to end it. The discussion

was suddenly interrupted by a sentry who rushed
in from the walls. 'Kings! Brothers!' he shouted,
'The Greeks are coming!'

Instantly Hector, the Trojan leader, son of
Priam, leapt to his feet and exclaimed, 'To your
posts! The meeting is adjourned! Be ready to
leave the city!' Immediately, they all rushed to
arm themselves, while the elderly, the women
and the children anxiously gathered on the walls.

The trumpets blared, the horses pawed the
ground, the ranks fell into line and the gates were
flung open, for Hector wanted to face the enemy
on the open field. One by one the bristling
divisions marched out and lined up for battle
around Thorn Hill – a lonely hillock which stood
out in the middle of the plain. The two entire
armies were on the field facing each other. Such
an array of forces had never been seen. The battle
which was about to begin was perhaps to decide
the fate of the war.

However, among the princes, one leader was
missing. Achilles, the most feared Greek and the
bravest, had remained in his tent.

BOOK III

As the two armies drew nearer to each other, Priam ordered Helen to meet him on the walls.

'You sent for me?' asked the beautiful woman for whom so much blood had been shed. 'What is it you wish, O Father and King?'

'I want you to show me one by one who the Greek leaders are. Who is that man with the shining armour who walks ahead of them all?'

'That is Agamemnon, my brother-in-law and overlord of the Greeks.'

'And those two men who lead such compact divisions, who are they? One is as tall as a giant, the other is shorter but broader in the shoulders.'

'The first one is the very powerful and most valiant Telamonian Aias. The other is Odysseus, King of Ithaca.'

From the walls of Troy, Priam and Helen watch the Greek army

Paris and Menelaus challenge each other to a duel to decide the fate of the war

'And that one, so noble and proud?' asked Priam again.

Troubled, Helen replied, 'That is Menelaus, my husband, from whom your son Paris abducted me.'

At that moment, Paris himself stepped forward from the Trojan ranks. Paris who had caused the war by abducting Helen, was very handsome in his flashing armour. He looked at the Greeks with arrogance, as though he wanted to defy them all. But when amongst them he noticed the tall figure of Menelaus, all his boldness disappeared. He halted, lowered his spear and meekly turned round to join his companions.

Hector, who had noticed all this, exclaimed with contempt, 'Paris! Aren't you ashamed of yourself? You walked high and mighty ahead of everyone, you seemed ready to take on the whole

Greek army by yourself, but when you saw Menelaus, your knees faltered and your heart quivered. Yet it is for you that we are fighting, don't you forget it!'

Hurt by these harsh words Paris replied, 'No, Brother! I shan't forget it. I admit I was frightened but it was only a fleeting moment of weakness. Listen to me: I shall go and challenge Menelaus to a duel. He and I alone will fight and so we shall decide the fate of the war. If he wins, return Helen to him and let the war be over. If I win, the Greeks must leave.'

Hector then ordered everyone to halt. In a clatter of arms and rising clouds of dust, the Trojans stopped, keeping in battle ranks. The Greeks also came to a halt. Agamemnon stepped forward on his own and shouted, 'Hector, what do you want? Why have you stopped? Do you want to surrender?'

14

'That you can never hope for, Agamemnon!' replied Hector, 'Paris is challenging your brother Menelaus to single combat! Greece on one side Troy on the other. The winner will decide the outcome of the war. Do you agree?'

Agamemnon agreed. And while the two armies stood motionless and silent in their ranks, Paris and Menelaus advanced towards each other. The Trojan war could well have ended there and then. Wielding their spears, the two men confronted each other. The first to strike was Paris. He threw his lance which whistled towards his opponent. Menelaus raised his shield and warded off the blow. Then in his turn, he launched his spear and struck his enemy's shield. At the same time, they both unsheathed their swords and went for each other. In the breathless silence only the clanging of the blades was heard. Paris was the younger and stronger of the two, but he was not as brave as Menelaus whose thirst for revenge swelled his heart and increased his strength. Menelaus struck with such fury that his sword shattered against Paris' shield.

A whisper rose from the spectators. Menelaus was disarmed, Paris could easily kill him. No. Before the young Trojan could move forward and strike, Menelaus lunged at him with his bare hands, caught him by his helmet and tugged at it with all his might. Paris tried to react but the strap was strangling him, the sword dropped from his hand, Menelaus pulled again and again till the strap broke and the Greek fell to the ground with the empty helmet in his arms. He jumped back to his feet, picked up his spear and with a cry leapt forward to stab his hated rival . . . but he was no longer there. Paris had vanished.

Aphrodite, the goddess of love, who had always protected the young Trojan prince, had protected him once more at this critical moment. She had surrounded him with a cloud of dust and had carried him off. Menelaus' spear sank into the ground.

Yet there was no doubt. The winner was the Greek. The Trojans could see that and withdrew in silence. Then Agamemnon moved forward and shouted, 'Greeks! Trojans! Hear me. You have all witnessed Menelaus' victory! According to our agreement Hector must return Helen to us, and may there now be peace!'

15

The gods meet to discuss Troy's destiny

BOOK IV

Whilst all this was taking place on the plain, the gods were once more conferring on Mount Olympus. Frowning, Zeus said, 'Athene and Hera to be sure, are on Menelaus' side, but they are content to watch and smile upon him. Whereas you Aphrodite, you descended to save Paris although he had been defeated and therefore deserved to perish. I am tired of this war. Let us put an end to it. Let us return Helen to Menelaus and let it be over!'

To this Hera replied, 'No, I don't want to see peace restored until Troy is destroyed!'

'What harm have Priam and his sons caused you that you want to see them all destroyed? Beware, Hera, if you want Troy to perish, perhaps one day I shall wipe out a city that is dear to you!'

'So be it! If that is your wish,' exclaimed the angry goddess. 'You can even destroy Athens or Sparta or Argos, my beloved cities. I shall not oppose your will, but do not oppose mine. Right now let them break the truce and resume combat. Athene it is up to you. Think of something! I want to see Troy destroyed.'

Athene swiftly left Olympus and descended to earth only a moment after Agamemnon had asked Hector to keep to the agreement. Assuming the appearance of a Trojan warrior, Laodocus, the goddess, came up to Pandarus, a very skilled archer who seldom missed his aim, and whispered to him, 'Pandarus, do not hesitate. If you love Troy, if you want to be honoured, if you want to win this war by yourself, then shoot! The time is right. Look, there is Menelaus still on his own where the duel took place. Kill him with an arrow. You can do it and you shall reap glory from it! The war is over! Do not hesitate!'

Pandarus was a man of honour and courage but Athene's words impressed and influenced him. Yes, the pacts had been solemnly drawn between Agamemnon and Hector but it would be worthwhile to break them if, with one arrow only, the war could be stopped and Troy saved.

Unseen, Pandarus notched a long arrow to his mighty bow, took aim, drew back the string, released it … The arrow was sent whistling through the air and would have pierced Menelaus' heart had not Athene – as quick as lightning – diverted it. The arrow hit the prince on his side, through the studded armour, cut the leather belt and sank into the flesh. Menelaus let out a brief cry and fell to his knees. Already the blood was spilling on to the earth. In a great uproar of fury and indignation the Greeks drew together brandishing their weapons.

'Treason! Treason!' they shouted, as Agamemnon bent over his brother lying on the ground.

'Fetch Machaon the doctor, tell him to be quick! In the meantime let us prepare! The Trojans will pay for this! No, brother,' he added seeing that Menelaus tried to pull out the arrow from his side, 'let Machaon tend to it. You shall not die from this wound and you shall fight again!'

Pandarus hits Menelaus with an arrow and so breaks the peace treaty

The other Greek princes rushed about while the whole army moved threateningly. The battle was about to start.

Meanwhile, a herald had hurriedly gone to fetch Machaon, son of Asclepius, the great physician. 'Come quickly,' he said, 'Menelaus has been wounded by an arrow. You must save him!'

Machaon tends the wounded Menelaus

Machaon hastened to the field where Menelaus lay, blood streaming from his wound. His friends had gathered close around him to protect and comfort him. Making his way through them, Machaon bent down, took a firm hold of the arrow and with a resolute pull removed it from the flesh.

'Do not fear, Menelaus,' he said, 'the wound is not as deep as you think.' Then he removed the prince's belt and armour, 'I can now dress your wound.'

'The enemy is coming!' someone shouted suddenly.

Indeed the Trojans, led by Hector, were advancing ready for the attack. Recovering from their bewilderment, the Trojans had reorganized their ranks for battle. They had hoped of course that the war would have been over with the outcome of the duel between Paris and Menelaus. Not everyone approved of Pandarus' action! But since the arrow had been shot and the blood had been shed and the peace treaty violated, it was clear that they must fight again. And fight they would for Troy must be defended at all cost, and although Paris was a cowardly warrior, it was worth fighting for a woman as beautiful as Helen.

'Forward, my friends!' Hector called out brandishing his sword. 'Our destiny lies in the battle!'

Hearing this Agamemnon unsheathed his shining sword and left Menelaus in the care of Machaon.

'Let the Trojans come, then! It is certainly not to the Trojans, who break peace treaties, that Zeus will lend his help!' he shouted. Before mounting his war chariot to which were harnessed two splendid, restless horses, the king passed his troops in review and addressed them thus: 'The time has come, sons of Greece! Here our fate will be decided! If we win we shall enter Troy, if we lose, the enemy will reach our camp, set fire to our ships and we shall lose all hope of sailing back to our country.'

'Odysseus, I am relying on you! Idomeneus, King of Crete, be strong in battle! Aias, son of Oïleus,' Agamemnon went on, 'Telamonian Aias, heroes, if I had more leaders as worthy as you the war would have been over long ago! Nestor, my friend, fight by my side! Diomedes, stand high on your chariot and strike boldly! Greeks, let's go! To battle!'

BOOK V

The two armies drew up opposite each other, led by the leaders standing tall on their chariots. As they marched the warriors shouted and shook their spears. Their shields glistened in the sun and the clang of arms rose to the sky. Even before the two armies met, showers of arrows rained down from the opposing ranks and some soldiers fell dead or wounded. But that did not stop the others. Like the wind-blown waves of the sea that come crashing down on the reef, retreating and surging forward with a mighty roar, so clashed the ranks of the Greeks and the Trojans. The latter had Athene against them and they knew it, but they also knew that Ares, the god of war, was on their side. In fact the gods, having come down from Olympus, took part in the battle, some to kill or spread terror, others to spare a life or give comfort to a dying man. Indeed, many of the warriors had a god as a mother or father. This was a war fought as much in heaven as on the plain which stretched out from the great walls of Troy and down to the sea.

Shields clashed against one another, spears crossed, iron-clad and leather-belted men came to blows, the air which had so-far echoed with shouts and insults, was now filled with moans and cries of lamentation, triumph or challenge. Voices of those dying and those killing, of the victors and of the defeated, mingled together. The first to fall was Phegeus, son of Dares, a young Trojan who was speared in the chest by Diomedes. Phegeus fell amidst a frightful clatter of bronze. Around his body the fury of the fight immediately intensified, because in this war, the dead were stripped of their weapons and it was a bitter disgrace to leave the corpse of a companion in the hands of the enemy.

It would be too lengthy to list all the princes, warriors or simple soldiers who met with death in that battle. It seemed that, after the first encounter, the Trojans were about to retreat under the enemy's assault, when Apollo's voice was heard above the din of the battle. 'Trojans, do not retreat! What do you fear? The flesh of the Greeks is not made of stone or iron that it cannot be wounded! Remember that today Achilles is not fighting! Forward! Forward!'

The Trojans counter-attacked and in the blood and the dust, the stamping of the horses and the squeaking of the chariots, under the rain of arrows and spears, there was Ares on the one side and Athene on the other jeering at each other. Weary, Athene suddenly called out, 'Ares, you who slaughter men in battle, come with me! Let us retire from the struggle, let us fight no more! Let us not anger our father, Zeus!' Thus speaking she took her violent brother by the hand and led him to the shore of the Scamander river. There they both came to a halt, panting and stained with blood.

The battle, though, continued to rage. Diomedes, one of the most valiant Greek princes, carried away with heroism flung himself on the Trojans with increasing fierceness, who, under his savage blows were again forced to draw back. Diomedes was like a stream in full spate, destroying everything and impossible to contain. But Pandarus, the same man who a little while ago had so treacherously wounded Menelaus, did not flinch at the sight of Diomedes. He notched an arrow to his mighty bow and did not miss his shot. The arrow struck Diomedes in the shoulder and he stopped and fell to his knees. A cheer of triumph rose and the Trojans resumed their attack. But the indomitable Diomedes fought back the pain and the weakness.

'Sthenelus', he ordered a companion, 'pull the arrow from my wound so that I may return to battle! And you Athene, give me back my strength and let me kill the man who has struck me!' The arrow was torn away and although he was losing blood, Diomedes went back into battle.

The field was red with blood and cluttered with fallen warriors. Two of Priam's sons, Chromius and Echemmon, who fought together in the same chariot were met by the enraged Diomedes. They were struck down, killed and stripped of their armour.

Then Aeneas, King of the Dardans and son of Aphrodite, summoned Pandarus. 'Pandarus,' he called out, 'we must stop Diomedes! Get on my chariot and let us away!'

Pandarus called as he came running, 'I have already struck the butcher now I shall kill him!

You drive the chariot, I'll take the spear.' They steered frantically across the battlefield in Diomedes' direction.

Sthenelus saw them coming and warned, 'Diomedes, fall back! Aeneas and Pandarus are coming for you! You are wounded, do not expose yourself!' Diomedes took no heed and fearlessly stood firm so that when Pandarus hurled the spear at him with all his might, he was ready to ward off the blow.

'He missed!' shouted Diomedes who retaliated with his spear. It stuck Pandarus through the throat and he fell dead from the chariot. Aeneas was ready to defend his friend's body, but Diomedes picked up a huge rock and hurled it at him, crushing his leg. Aeneas sank to his knees and would certainly have died by the bloody spear of his enemy, had not Aphrodite come to his rescue, hiding him under a fold of her veil. But not even a goddess could stop Diomedes, who shouting, ran in hot pursuit of Aphrodite and cut her wrist with his spear.

The beautiful goddess screamed with pain and the warrior bawled, 'Off with you! This is war and if you wanted to see what it was like, now you know!'

In a whirlwind, Aphrodite returned to Olympus weeping. She was shaken and bloodstained but she had saved her beloved son Aeneas from certain death.

Diomedes strength came from Athene who, after getting her breath back, had gone once more into the battle. Immediately, Ares had followed her, rushing to the aid of the Trojans.

'How much longer will you allow this massacre to continue?' he called out to them. 'Aeneas is wounded. Perhaps you want to leave him in the hands of the enemy?'

Roused by these words, the Trojans made a desperate counter-attack. Hector led on his chariot, opening their way into the enemy until he reached Aeneas and snatched him from the Greeks. Although in a sorry state, Aeneas was still able to fight. But once again the Trojans

The battle between Trojans and Greeks rages on furiously

were compelled to retreat and found themselves driven back under the walls of Troy.

One of Priam's sons, the valiant Helenus, who had fought all day on the frontline, approached Hector and said, 'Brother, things are getting bad. We have not yet lost but the gates of Troy are so close that someone might be tempted to take refuge inside the city – and that would be a disaster. You and Aeneas must tell the men to carry on fighting and they will fight. But Hector, this is not enough. You must go into the city and ask the older women to make an offering to Athene of a robe, the loveliest they can find. She must cease to be our enemy!'

Hector assented and with Aeneas by his side he rode to the frontline, rousing his men's fighting spirit and urging them to resist. Then he rushed inside the city of Troy through a door that was opened for him.

Hecuba and the Trojan ladies make an offering to Athene of their most precious robe

BOOK VI

Bloodstained, covered in dust and drenched in perspiration under his dented armour, Hector reached Priam's royal palace. He was climbing up the stairs when Hecuba his mother, came rushing to him.

'Hector, my son, have you come to pray to Zeus so that he will support us in battle? Yes, you must! But first drink this wine, it will refresh you. You are tired, I can see it!'

'No, noble mother, do not offer me wine. I dare not drink to Zeus with my hands covered in blood. And wine robs a man of his strength. But listen to me. Collect your daughters, your daughters-in-law and the noble ladies of Troy and take your most precious robe to Athene as a gift.

Promise her that every year we shall sacrifice to her twelve of the best cows in the land. Pray she may keep Diomedes away from battle. He is the one who is destroying us! Do it now, Mother! I am going to look for Paris!'

Having spoken, Hector hastened through the corridors and the splendid rooms of the palace. Shortly after, Hecuba together with the other women, solemnly laid before Athene's statue, the most richly embroidered robe she possessed. She promised the wrathful goddess numerous and generous sacrifices.

'O, Goddess,' prayed the Trojan women, 'break the spear of Diomedes, the slaughterer.' But it was to no avail; Athene shook her head.

22

Meanwhile Hector reached Helen's quarters. There he found Paris sitting peacefully by his beautiful wife, quietly polishing his helmet, armour and shield.

'Shame on you!' Hector shouted reproachfully. 'Our men are falling all around the city because of you, and what do you do? You polish these weapons you don't even have the courage to use! Off with you, rascal, run to your post and fight!'

'Hector, my brother,' replied Paris blushing, 'yes you are right, you all fight and I remain inside, but be patient, try to understand me. I was only seeking comfort at Helen's side. Anyway she has urged me to return to the front. I shall only be a moment, then I shall put on my armour and join you!'

Then Helen spoke. 'Hector, I would rather be dead than be the cause of this war! I have tried to convince Paris to fight, but his heart is what it is! Come and sit by me, brother-in-law, rest awhile and ...'

Hector reproaches Paris, who instead of fighting, idles by Helen's side

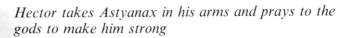
Hector takes Astyanax in his arms and prays to the gods to make him strong

'I cannot Helen!' interrupted Hector. 'The Trojans are struggling and they need me. I wish to see my wife and son. You see to it that Paris gets ready and goes back to his post. This is a decisive day which might bring the end of us!' And Hector left to find his wife, Andromache.

But she was not in her rooms, nor with Hecuba and the other women making the offerings to Athene's statue. Having heard that the Greeks were winning, she had taken with her a maid and her little son Astyanax and had rushed to the walls and climbed up the tower over the Scaean Gate which overlooked the battlefield. So to the Scaean gate Hector hastened. When Andromache saw him, she ran into his arms, pale and distraught.

As Hector looked at Astyanax and smiled, she whispered, 'Ah, you unfortunate man! This bravery of yours will be the end of you! Have you no pity for me, Hector, nor for your little son? I have nobody else in the world but you. You are to me a husband, father, mother and brother. Have mercy on us, stay here in the tower! Rally the army from inside the city without going out to battle!'

'I should like to, wife,' replied Hector thoughtfully, 'but I cannot fail in my duty. Perhaps I shall die, but at least you will be proud to have been the wife of a fighter who did not take flight.' Then he added softly, 'Give me the child!' He took Astyanax in his arms, who terrified by his father's countenance and his helmet let out a childish wail.

The hero smiled and took his helmet off. He kissed his son and said, 'Zeus and you other gods, grant me that this boy of mine may grow strong and reign over Troy. Many people say he is stronger than his father!'

Then handing the boy back to his wife, he went on, 'Do not weep Andromache. If my fate is to live no one can kill me. But death awaits us all, cowards and heroes alike and no one can escape it. Be brave!' As he spoke he put on his helmet and left the fair Andromache in tears. He came down from the tower and headed for the gate. On his way he met Paris dressed for battle, and together they rejoined their army.

24

BOOK VII

As soon as both men had resumed their posts, the Trojans took courage and pressed forward. At their unexpected counter-attack the Greeks drew back. From the heights of Mount Olympus where the weary Athene had retired, she saw what was happening. She swiftly took off for Troy and had barely set foot on earth when she met Apollo.

'Athene, why have you flown down from Olympus once again? Are you keen to see Troy sacked? Listen to me: too much blood has been shed. Let us unite and put an end to this massacre. They will fight again to be sure, but it is enough for today.'

'Yes, Apollo,' replied the goddess, 'I also feel that it is enough for today. But how can we stop the men fighting?'

'There is a way. Let us make Hector challenge one of the Greek princes to a duel. That way the battle will cease.'

Athene and Apollo talk of a way to stop the fighting

The two children of Zeus agreed and induced Helenus to speak the following words to his brother Hector, 'Hear me, Hector, I don't know what has come over me but I feel certain that you shall not die today. Have our men sit down and order them to stop fighting. Then go forward alone and challenge a Greek to a duel.'

Hector agreed. Pacing up and down in front of his troops he commanded the men to cease fighting and sit down on the ground. Seeing the Trojans laying down their arms and sit in orderly ranks, Agamemnon immediately gave the same order to the Greeks. A great silence fell where only a short while earlier battle had raged. Everyone was now still where before there had been a frenzied turmoil of men and chariots. Hector stepped forward and stood between the two armies.

'Hear me all! The outcome of this war is victory or death. I am here to challenge any Greek who is prepared to fight me! This is my proposal and may Zeus be my witness. The victor will strip the other of his arms but must send the corpse back so that he may be given a warrior's burial. Come now! Who will accept my challenge?'

A long silence followed these words. Hector was a great warrior and he fought to defend his country. No Greek was then willing to take up such a challenge.

The long embarassed silence lasted till old Nestor exclaimed, 'Oh, shame on you Greeks. Can it be that not one of you will step forward? If I were young, I would take on Hector!'

At the old man's words nine Greek princes stood up, their faces red with shame. They were

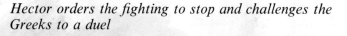

Hector orders the fighting to stop and challenges the Greeks to a duel

Hector and Aias Telamonian draw their swords and fight against each other

Agamemnon, Diomedes, Aias (son of Oïleus), Telamonian Aias, Idomeneus, Meriones, Odysseus, Eurypylus and Thoas; all ready for the duel. A draw was to pick Hector's opponent. Fate chose Telamonian Aias, the tallest and strongest of the Greeks. When Hector saw him advancing, clad in bronze with his vast shield, wielding his spear and with a threatening sneer on his face, he felt nervous. But to have withdrawn then would have meant eternal shame for him. So he stood firm and waited.

'Hector,' shouted Aias, stopping at some distance, 'you see that although Achilles is not amongst us today, we can still fight. You go first and begin the duel.'

'So be it Aias and let it be an open fight!' As he spoke Hector launched his spear which planted itself into Aias' shield with a heavy thud. Aias retaliated by piercing Hector's shield with his spear. Having no more spears, the two heroes began to hurl great boulders at each other.

Struck and wounded in the neck, Hector staggered to his knees, but Apollo quickly helped him up again. Drawing their swords, the rivals closed in on each other and would have fought relentlessly until death, had not two heralds, a Greek and a Trojan, come up and separated them.

'Enough, valiant warriors,' they said, 'Stop the fighting. You are both brave and both loved by Zeus. Enough, it is nearly dark!'

'So be it Aias!' said Hector. 'We have struck each other many blows, let us now exchange gifts so that it may be said by all, these two have fought each other fiercely but they have parted friends!' With this he handed his opponent his sword and received Aias' valuable purple belt. So ended the duel.

There was no more fighting on that day. The remaining hours before sunset were devoted to the sad task of gathering and burying with all the honours the warriors who had fallen in combat.

BOOK VIII

Another day began. On Mount Olympus, Zeus summoned all the gods to a conference. His face was sombre. 'Listen to me all, and listen well. I shall tell you what I think and let none of you contradict me. What is happening in Troy is worrying and annoying me. It must end. I won't have any of you going down to help either the Greeks or the Trojans. I have spoken many times before but you have taken no notice. Well, if I see any one of you, whoever it is, flying down to earth to meddle in this wretched war, I shall strike him with my lightning. Then you will know the wrath of Zeus.'

With this, Zeus mounted his chariot and flew off to Mount Ida from where he could survey the battlefield. Impressed, the gods dared not move and remained on Olympus, silent and thoughtful.

Meanwhile, at sunrise, Greeks and Trojans had taken up their arms again and were preparing for another battle. Soon the converging forces met and the same bloody scenes repeated themselves. More dead, more suffering, more heroes fell to the ground and were stripped of their arms. The fight lasted through the morning, until at last Zeus brought out the Scales of Fortune. He placed the Greeks' fate on one plate and the Trojans' fate on the other. The latter felt heavier which meant that Fortune was on the Trojans' side.

Zeus immediately sent a flash of lightning down among the Greek troops, who, terrified by the deafening blast, scattered in all directions with the enemy following at their heels. During the retreat, old Nestor alone lingered behind, and would have been easy prey for the Trojans but for Diomedes, who noticed him. He steered his chariot round and whipping the horses furiously drove to his rescue.

On his chariot, Zeus goes to Mount Ida to watch the battlefield

Zeus sends a bolt of lightning to earth which falls in front of Diomedes' chariot

'Where are you running to, Greeks?' he shouted as he rode. 'Are you fleeing too Odysseus? Won't you come and help me to rescue Nestor?' His words were lost in the turmoil and alone, he drew up to the old man, lept off the chariot and helped Nestor on to it.

'We shall not flee, Nestor,' he said. 'Though you are old I shall take you to battle and Hector will see who we are. Sthenelus!' he ordered his faithful charioteer, 'Head straight for Hector!'

So in the general flight, Diomedes returned alone to the attack, aiming his spear at Hector's heart. He missed but instead struck the Trojan hero's charioteer. Zeus then intervened once more and with a terrific thunderclap he flashed a dazzling bolt to earth, right in front of Diomedes' chariot. The frightened horses neighed and reared, and Nestor shouted, 'Ah! Diomedes! I fear this is a sign from the gods! Zeus is against us! Let us withdraw!'

'I shall not withdraw! Let no one say that I was afraid!'

'Indeed, no one who knows you shall ever dare

to say that, Diomedes,' replied Nestor worriedly. 'But do not defy the wrath of Zeus again!'

Finally the chariot was steered round in the dust and driven back to the Greek camp, while the Trojans, taking courage, pressed forward with a terrific roar, led by Hector who urged them from his chariot.

'Trojans, allies, friends! Yesterday Fortune was not on our side but today we shall win! If our fighting spirit holds, today we shall invade the Greek camp and end the war! Go! Do not linger! As Diomedes flees we shall go after him! Forward!'

They all followed him and not one Greek warrior dared to turn round and face them. It was indeed a terrible downfall. Never had the Greeks fled in this manner before. One by one or in disorderly groups they scrambled across the trench which protected their camp and took refuge behind the wall that surrounded it. The Trojans kept at their heels relentlessly, bombarding them with arrows and spears. In short, not one Greek remained outside the wall.

It was a strong and well-built wall with solid ramparts that protected the Greek camp, the tents, the headquarters and the ships which were nearly all dry-docked along the shore. The ships were for the Greeks an indispensable element in the war, because if they were lost they could not get weapon and war supply reinforcements. But losing the ships would mean an even greater disaster: without the ships how could they sail back to their homeland?

Intent as they were to reach the wall, the Trojans hadn't looked at the sky, they hadn't realized that the sun had completed its course and was setting. When the shadows of night fell with a long gust of wind, Hector was taken aback and shocked. He turned to the sea reddened by sunset. Stopping in his tracks, he halted his troops and shouted, 'Enough, brothers! Stop here! I hoped to assail the enemy ships but soon it will be dark. We must respect the night and stop fighting! It does not matter,' he added, 'this time we shall not withdraw, we shall not return to the city, we shall not leave this ground that we have conquered. Send a messenger to tell our wives and friends that the army will stay on the field. The Greeks,' he went on, pointing at the wall, 'cannot escape us. Tomorrow at dawn we shall break through their defences and set fire to their ships. When they have lost their means of retreat they will also lose heart to fight. You will see! Nobody in the world will ever dare to make war on Troy! Let us pitch camp and light huge fires. From those fires we shall take the flames which tomorrow will burn down the enemy ships!'

Hector orders his men to pitch camp and light fires. They will spend the night on conquered land instead of going back to the city

Nestor reproaches Agamemnon for having quarrelled with Achilles

BOOK IX

Inside their camp that night, the Greeks could not sleep as they were worried. The sentries paced the ramparts, silently watching the fires as they were lit by the Trojans, and listening to their songs of victory.

The Greek princes were holding a meeting in Agamemnon's tent. Never in nine years of war had they suffered such a bitter defeat. 'I had not suspected such fighting fury from the Trojans,' mumbled Agamemnon disheartened. 'I really didn't know they had it in them. It must be a sign from the heavens. Zeus is telling us that we shall never take Troy!'

'Do not speak so! We shall take Troy even if I must do it alone with my charioteer Sthenelus!' replied Diomedes harshly.

Old Nestor intervened, 'It is not with words that one fights. Agamemnon you are discouraged and it is understandable, but remember we are battling without Achilles, and without his mighty arm – like it or not – we cannot hope to win. I shall be frank with you, you have offended him, it is now up to you to make peace with him.'

After a moment of silence Agamemnon whispered, 'Yes, I admit I have offended Achilles. He has refused to fight and that is the cause of our

31

In his tent, Achilles plays the lyre while Patroclus listens silently

defeat. Friends,' he went on, 'I know I was wrong, but I am your king and leader. Hear then what I have to say to you and I hope that by tomorrow Achilles will go back to battle.'

Soon after, Nestor, Aias and Odysseus left Agamemnon's tent and walking along the seashore headed towards Achilles' campsite, well guarded by the Myrmidons of the long spears.

Achilles was in his tent with his good friend Patroclus. They were unarmed and their armour, shields, leggings and helmets stood in a corner of the tent. Sitting on a bench, Achilles was playing his lyre, humming ancient songs which told of war and heroic feats, while Patroclus listened in silence. It was as though they were a thousand miles away from Troy and the bloody battlefield, but in Achilles' heart anger and contempt still burnt.

At the sight of Nestor, Aias and Odysseus, the young man at once put down his lyre, stood to his feet with a smile and stretched out his arms.

'Friends!' he exclaimed, 'What a joy it is to see you again! Come! And you Patroclus, pour us some of the reddest and purest wine! Odysseus, Aias, wise Nestor! Drink and eat with me!'

And so they ate and drank and talked as though nothing had happened in the past few days. At last raising his cup to Achilles, Odysseus said, 'Friend, it is not only to drink that we have come. We have just been holding a conference in Agamemnon's tent. Achilles, glory of all Greece, Agamemnon has sent us to tell you that he admits to his error, he admits that he has offended you by taking away Briseis from you, whom you had well deserved by your courage. If you will go back to battle he is ready to return her to you. Not only that but when Troy is sacked you will have the privilege of choosing twenty slaves from among the most beautiful Trojan maidens and when we sail back to Greece you may marry one of Agamemnon's daughters. You will be Achilles, son-in-law of the king of all Greeks. This we have come to tell you. We are asking you to fight again.'

Odysseus had spoken. He was now quiet. A long silence followed and Achilles replied in a low tone, 'Odysseus you have been frank with me, so I shall be frank with you. You have been sent by the man I hate more than anyone in the world. He had my trust, he has lost it. He had my friendship, he has lost it. He has shown that he possessed neither generosity nor loyalty. I have served him faithfully and as a reward he has taken away my precious Briseis, the girl whom I loved. Agamemnon will never be able to convince me of his change of heart. He sent you to me not because he has understood that he was unfair, but only because he has suffered a bitter defeat on the battleground. Let him fight on alone against Hector. Anyway,' the young man went on, 'I shall soon be off, I shall soon be leaving this land where I certainly never came of my own free will!'

'Achilles ...' Odysseus began to say, but Achilles continued, 'My mother Thetis, hearing that I was leaving for Troy, told me that by coming here to fight I would find death and with it eternal glory, and she added that if I did not take part in the war, my life would instead be a long and happy one. Well I have changed my mind. I now choose a long and happy life and I advise you all to do the same. It is useless to carry on. You will never conquer Troy.'

An astounded silence followed these words. Odysseus and his companions tried in vain to convince Achilles to change his mind. So after they had drunk a last cup of wine, the three of them went back to Agamemnon with the bitter answer. Achilles was not giving in, he was still angered. He would not return to fight.

Achilles does not give in to Nestor's plea and refuses to return to battle

Odysseus and Diomedes meet Dolon on his way to spy on their camp

BOOK X

In the still of night the soldiers exhausted by their day of fighting had laid down on the ground to rest and sleep. But not all were asleep. Anxiety kept Agamemnon awake. The Trojans had stirred along the wall not far from the ships. What were they up to? They would surely attack, but when? Tonight? Tomorrow?

Never had Hector come so close. With a sombre face Agamemnon watched the many fires the Trojans had lit on the plain. The danger was great and the Greeks might well be doomed to disaster.

At last the king came to a decision. He could no longer contain his anguish and so went to each of the leaders' tents and called them out one by one for yet another war meeting.

'It is necessary,' he began, 'to know what the Trojans' intentions are, whether they will attack tonight or wait until tomorrow. Our troops are tired and most of them are asleep. We must know if we can let them sleep or if we must line them up for battle.'

Odysseus and Diomedes volunteered to go and spy on the Trojans. Stealthily they crept out through a small door in the wall and walking silently across the plain littered with corpses and weapons, they came close to the enemy fires. Suddenly Odysseus held back his companion, and whispered, 'Stop! I think I can hear someone coming.'

He was right, a shadow appeared out of the darkness and they saw the glint of armour. Diomedes leapt forward brandishing his spear. 'Stop!' he shouted. 'Who goes there?'

34

The man stopped and fearfully implored, 'Don't harm me, spare me!'

'Who are you? Speak up if you don't want to die where you stand!'

'My name is Dolon. Hector sent me. I was told to creep into your camp,' replied the man with a trembling voice. 'To find out what you were doing, whether you were going to fight again or were preparing to leave.'

'Ah! So you think you have defeated us once and for all? No, Dolon we are not leaving. But speak up, have you perhaps received reinforcements to feel so sure of yourselves?'

Dolon, who had accepted the spying mission to the Greek camp only because he had been offered a handsome reward, replied, 'Yes. The Thracians have come led by their young King Rhesus. They are camping over there on the right. Rhesus,' he added, 'owns two beautiful white horses, the loveliest I have ever seen. But please let me go, I . . .' He was not able to finish his sentence, Diomedes had struck him a fatal blow with his sword. 'If that one had reported back to Hector, we would have been done for,' he explained. 'But come Odysseus let us bid welcome to the Thracians!'

They walked on and reached the Trojan camp. Some soldiers were armed, others were asleep. The two heroes slipped unseen and noiselessly towards the still tents and headed for the enclosure where several horses slept. Yes, Dolon had spoken the truth. The two big thoroughbreds were certainly the most handsome creatures ever seen under the walls of Troy! Ah, if only they could take them back to their camp as loot, what a boast it would be!

'I'll take care of the beasts,' whispered Odysseus, 'you take care of the men.'

Diomedes nodded and moved stealthily towards a huge tent. Meanwhile, Odysseus, crawling on the ground, reached the enclosure and found a way in. He moved slowly and cautiously among the horses so that they wouldn't feel his presence and start to paw and whinny. He had reached the splendid white horses that belonged to King Rhesus!

Odysseus takes hold of Rhesus' two splendid white horses

35

At that moment Diomedes had penetrated the Thracian quarters. As soon as they had arrived, the Thracians had retired to bed in order to be fresh for the next day's battle. It was indeed ill luck to have joined at a moment of victory. Ill luck because feeling very bold and sure of themselves they had not even remembered to put out sentries to watch over the camp.

The terrible Diomedes unsheathed his sword and, since in times of war any action which can harm the enemy and undermine his strength is fully justified, one by one he killed at least twelve warriors in their sleep – among whom was the young King Rhesus, who had come to Troy hoping to find glory and was instead slaughtered like a lamb. Diomedes would have continued his massacre had he not feared someone might wake up and raise the alarm. Thinking that Odysseus had already got hold of the horses, he decided to return, his sword still dripping with blood. Odysseus was waiting impatiently for him to return.

'Quick! The Trojans are everywhere! If they find us, all is lost!'

'At least twelve of them, and Rhesus among them, will never find out anything,' replied Diomedes with a sneer. 'Come, let's take the chariot and leave!'

They harnessed the two horses to Rhesus' chariot, lashed the animals on and made their way back to the Greek camp. Their screams and the noise of the hooves woke the Thracian soldiers who discovered the men slaughtered in their sleep. The alarm was promptly raised and all the Trojan princes and Hector came running. Alas, it was too late; Rhesus lay dead in a pool of his own blood, and the cloud of dust visible in the night showed that his murderers were in full flight taking with them the two splendid horses.

Such was war. They weep on one side, they rejoice on the other. So the Trojan camp was in mourning whilst the Greeks celebrated Odysseus' and Diomedes' mission with wine and song.

After having harnessed the two horses to Rhesus' chariot, Odysseus and Diomedes head back to camp

BOOK XI

At last dawn broke. Their strength restored by night, the Greeks prepared to counter-attack. They must drive back the enemy as far as possible away from the ships. Therefore they must leave the camp in force to go to battle.

As on the previous day and many other times during the nine long years, the troops in battle array, clashed. Once more chariots were driven furiously at soldiers, once more brave young men challenged each other, met in combat, killed or were killed. Once more the arid land drank the heroes' blood.

Never had Agamemnon fought so gallantly, never had he struck and killed so many enemies. It seemed that nobody could fight him and already some of the Trojans were retreating under his repeated assaults, when Coön (son of Antenor) suddenly confronted him and speared his arm. Howling with rage and pain Agamemnon turned round and killed his assailant, but was no longer able to hold up his shield against the hail of arrows. He could do nothing but drag himself to his chariot and withdraw.

'Agamemnon is fleeing!' Hector shouted. 'Attack now!' It was now the Greeks turn to fall back. Many in fact dropped their weapons in order to run faster. Diomedes who had fought alongside Odysseus, cursed and shouted, 'What in heavens are you doing, fleeing like sheep? Have you lost your strength all at once? Stay with me Odysseus, let us resist!'

In answering him, Odysseus exclaimed, 'I shall not run Diomedes, I shall stay by you and fight. But I am convinced that Zeus has again come to the Trojans' rescue and that there is very little hope left for us.'

However, both warriors turned their menacing faces towards the enemy and stood their ground. Hector rushed up to attack them but was grazed by a spear and forced to retreat. Mocking him Diomedes shouted 'Ha, you run Hector! But wherever you are I shall find you and I will make you fight to the end!'

Agamemnon is hurt in the arm by a spear

From the stern of the ship Achilles watches the various stages of the battle

He had barely ended his sentence when Paris shot an arrow which sank deep into Diomedes' right foot. Pain-stricken Diomedes stopped, cursing. The triumphant Paris gloated over him, 'You have been hit. I only wish I had been accurate and hit you in the stomach!'

'Damned fool!' replied Diomedes. 'I should like to see you without your bow, sword to sword! You wouldn't talk like this then!'

But already the Trojans were closing in on him, and he could not move, neither to defend himself nor to run. This time he would have been lost without Odysseus' intervention, who shielded him and carried on fighting single-handed against a hundred Trojans. He killed many but in the fierce fighting was unable to avoid a spear, thrown at him by Socus, son of Hippasus. The tremendous blow would have been fatal if Athene had not softened it.

Odysseus knew that he could not hold on much longer. Soon he would be forced to yield and it would mean death for him and for Diomedes. He then started shouting for help and through the din of the battle his cries reached Menelaus' ears who exclaimed, 'Odysseus needs help! Aias come with me, quick! Away we go!'

The battle rages on and turns in favour of the Trojans

Both dashed forward and found Odysseus covered in blood defending himself against a horde of enemies. Aias stepped in front of him using his gigantic shield to give them shelter. Behind this shelter, Menelaus was able to take Odysseus and Diomedes back to safety. Drained of all strength Menelaus had to help them on to the chariot before he could drive them back to the camp.

And so the Trojan onslaught continued, led by Hector and Paris. Paris, in keeping with his promise to the beautiful Helen, was trying to cancel the unimpressive proof of courage he had shown in battle until now. One after another, he sent vicious arrows from his bow inflicting death or painful wounds. One of them struck Machaon, the physician, which was a severe blow to the Greeks.

'Nestor!' shouted Idomeneus to the old warrior who was always present on the frontline, 'Machaon is worth a hundred men! Help him on to your chariot and take him to a shelter! We'll cover you!' As this was carried out the battle continued to rage, turning in favour of the Trojans who, step by step, moved toward the wall which protected the Greek tents and ships.

High above, at the stern of his ship resting on dry land, Achilles watched. Unperturbed, he had followed the various stages of the battle but now called to his loyal friend Patroclus and said, 'Patroclus, Nestor is driving a wounded man out of the battlefield. I cannot make out who it is but it looks like Machaon. Go and find out. Machaon is dear to me, he is a friend that I should never wish to lose.'

Patroclus set off running and found Nestor in his tent applying first aid treatment to Machaon who was in a bad state.

'Why is Achilles so concerned about Machaon?' exclaimed the old man. 'Many other Greeks have been wounded! Diomedes has been wounded, and so has Odysseus, and Agamemnon! ... We have reached our limit and what does he do? He watches us die!'

'He has been too deeply offended,' replied Patroclus, 'he won't fight.'

Nestor shook his white head and mumbled, 'This will be the end of us all. You Patroclus show that you are truly his friend and ask him to come to our rescue! And if he won't, then ask him to give you his weapons and come in his place! The Trojans will mistake you for Achilles, and daunted, they might relent!'

Patroclus dared not answer and ran back to Achilles' tent. Along the way he saw nothing but wounded men, worn out and resigned to defeat.

BOOK XII

So the Trojans pursued the Greeks who at first retreated beyond the trench and then clambered over their camp wall. From the top of it a hail of arrows rained on the attackers. In the dust and tumult the Trojans' chariots came to a halt, lining up along the edge of the trench which was strewn with bodies. Some charioteers pushed forward and tried to overcome the obstacle but the horses reared and neighed in fright at the sight of the ditch. It was impossible to drive them over.

'Hector!' shouted Polydamas, one of the bravest Trojans. 'It is senseless trying to cross the ditch with our chariots, let us leave them and cross on foot. If the Greeks attack us while we are in the chariots we are done for!'

'Yes!' Hector agreed, 'On foot! Forward!' and he leapt from his chariot. Never before had

The fight intensifies under the wall without allowing one moment's rest

victory seemed so close at hand. The ships were near and so were the supplies and arms storehouse. To loot and sack them would be to strike a fatal blow at the Greeks. Leading his men Hector crossed the trench on foot and reached the wall. There was a ceaseless and deadly exchange of arrows, stones and spears.

Protecting themselves with their shields, the Trojans moved forward to a reinforced gate which was being defended by the desperate Greek soldiers who knew full well that if they yielded all would be lost for them. Even those men, who, exhausted by the long struggle had needed to get their breath back, rest awhile and tend to their wounds, fought on relentlessly. There was no time left, this was a struggle for life and it did not tolerate one moment's rest.

Suddenly someone screamed 'The sky! Look at the sky!' They all looked up. Flying in the sky directly above the battlefield was a great eagle holding in its talons an enormous snake. The

snake, far from being dead, was writhing and hissing and trying to break free or pay dearly for its life. With a desperate contortion it lifted its head and sank its sharp fangs into the eagle's breast. Viciously bitten the great bird let out a shrill cry of pain, withdrew its talons and dropped its prey. The snake fell to the ground and slithered away. Polydamas, though brave that he was, turned pale.

'The snake is a sign from Zeus, Hector,' he said. 'I see it as an ill omen. I think Zeus is telling us that we will reach the ships but that the Greeks will harm us – seriously.'

'What are you saying, Polydamas?' exclaimed Hector. 'Do you think I care about eagles and snakes? I believe in battle only, and we are winning it! Are you afraid to fight, are you afraid to die? Beware, if you are thinking of retiring I shall be the one to kill you! Forward! Attack the gate! Trojans, let us knock it down!'

The commanding Hector led his men into attack, looking for a suitable place to make an opening through the wall. As it shook under the rocks thrown by the Trojans, so trembled the Greeks' hearts who continued defending themselves with lances, stones and arrows.

In the sky appears a great eagle holding an enormous snake trying to free itself

41

Hector seizes a large rock and hurls it against the gate

'Lycians, my valorous men, here! Stand by my side! With me! I cannot breach the wall on my own! Where is your courage? Why aren't you behind me? Forward! If we all unite, no one can resist us!'

Against the Lycians' massive onslaught Teucer's arrows and Aias' deadly spear had no effect. Both had to withdraw and, following Sarpedon, the Lycians at last hoisted themselves up on the wall with shouts of triumph. The battle became fiercer. Reinforcement battalions were sent in from both sides to join the battle. There was not a Greek or Trojan prince who was not spattered with blood, either his own or that of his enemy's, and yet there was no way of telling on which side victory was leaning. Suddenly out of the clangour and over the din of the battle, Hector's thundering voice rose 'Horse-tamer Trojans! Down with the wall, let us reach the ships and set them alight!'

All united in a supreme effort. Driven by an incredible strength, Hector seized a massive pointed boulder – so heavy that it would have been difficult for two men to lift – and hurled it against the gate, hitting the two iron bars which held its panels together. The colossal hinges shook, the iron bars gave way and the two panels shattered into splinters. A roar of triumph rose from the Trojans who at last saw the opening through which they would invade the enemy camp. The first one to leap forward was naturally Hector who held two spears in his hands. No one dared to confront him and anyhow no one would hold him now.

'Follow me! Follow me!' he shouted, turning to the men behind him, and already more gates were giving way. Here and there the wall was dotted with Trojans who had climbed over it, breaking the enemy's resistance and swarming the ramparts. Through the shattered gates, through the breaches, the Trojans poured into the Greek camp like a mighty river that had burst its banks and was flooding the plain.

There was nothing left for the Greeks to do but to retreat to the ships. More than a retreat, it was flight! The Greeks were unable to organize a line of defence and they were unable to halt and regroup. It seemed then that nothing could save the ships, and consequently the whole Greek army, from destruction and catastrophe.

Then forward stepped Sarpedon, leader of the Lycian warriors who had given their support to the Trojans. Protected by a large shield, Glaucus, another Lycian prince, walked by his side. Behind them followed close ranks of warriors. Telemonian Aias and his brother Teucer rushed to oppose them. From the ramparts, which the Lycians had begun to scale, Teucer repelled Glaucus with an arrow, but Sarpedon stood firm. Zeus himself protected him. When Aias launched his spear with his usual outstanding power, it embedded itself full into the Lycian prince's shield, but didn't pierce through. Sarpedon, however, staggered under the blow, his arm numbed. This weakness lasted but a second and inspired by Zeus he recovered.

BOOK XIII

But something happened up in the heavens. Zeus, who had been watching the Trojan offensive, at last turned his gaze away from the battlefield. He was satisfied that in obeying his orders, none of the gods had interfered in the battles. There was no doubt then that Hector and his men would get to the ships. There was no need for him to remain any longer. The gods' father therefore boarded his resplendent carriage and drove off to visit the land of the horse-breeding Thracians.

He had barely gone, when Poseidon hastened to the battlefield, waving his trident. He was determined to bring help to the Greeks whom he favoured. He could not accept their destruction, he could not bear to watch them so, retreating and falling.

As Zeus leaves on his chariot, Poseidon hastens to the Greeks' rescue

Peisander and Menelaus confront each other in a fierce duel

Amongst the scampering Greek troops, he assumed the appearance of Calchas and accosted Telamonian Aias and Aias of Oïleus and shouted to both, 'There is in you enough power to save the whole army! What is the matter with you? Why do you think in terms of defeat and not of victory? Do not stay here. To battle, go back to battle!'

And with these words he tapped the two warriors with his magic staff lending them ardour and heroic spirit. The Trojans who pressed their advance further towards the ships suddenly met a counter attack. Until then the Trojan army had behaved like a boulder hurtling down a mountain, leaping wildly from rock to rock, mowing down everything on its path. But now, once it had reached the plain it was like it had lost its momentum and had slowly come to a halt. So the Trojans halted before the Greeks, who influenced by the two Aias' were displaying renewed resistance.

In the bloody encounters that followed, many heroes fell on both sides, and over their bodies the struggle continued furiously. They fought in various places, under the ships' sterns. They fought with spears and swords, chariots clashed, the ground was cluttered with the dead and the moaning wounded. The earth was drenched with blood, littered with shattered spears, broken arrows, shields, helmets which had been torn off warriors' heads, lances that had not reached their target. Duels were fought between heroes, entire divisions of roaring soldiers came to grips with each other and in the chaos and heat of the combats, it was difficult to distinguish one's enemy from one's friend.

44

It was a glorious day for Idomeneus, King of the Cretans, who fought alongside the Greeks. But it was also a great day for Deiphobus, Priam's son and also for Aeneas, and for Paris and for the other Trojans. Supported by Poseidon, the Greeks were fighting bravely, and now that Zeus was looking elsewhere and was no longer keeping an eye on the battle, the Trojans suffered painful losses. In the battle Menelaus was tackled by young Peisander. Their vibrating spears drew no result, so they grasped their swords and engaged in a fierce exchange of blows and Peisander was killed.

Everywhere the wavering Trojan lines were driven back. Harpalion, prince of the Paphlagonians, allies of Troy, was struck dead by an arrow. He was immediately avenged by Paris who shot Euchenor, King of Corinth, with his unerring bow. On the whole, the left wing of the Trojan army was retreating.

Polydamas then ran in search of Hector who was fighting on the right wing. 'Hector,' he called out, 'we must call our troops or we will have fought in vain. There is no strategy in our attack!'

'You are right,' replied Hector, leaping from his chariot, 'stay here while I go to the left wing and give them orders!'

Hector's presence and voice restored new life to the Trojans. They reassembled to face the enemy frontline who stopped in their tracks. Hector dashed incessantly up and down the front ranks. Aias, upon seeing him, made his way through the soldiers and defied him.

'Hector!' he roared. 'Where do you think you are going? To our ships? You are mistaken. You will not get through! Only one path is open to you, that is the path of flight!'

'No Aias,' replied Hector, 'I shall not flee. Instead, this day shall be the Greeks' last! And yours too if you stand in my way! Before nightfall the dogs and the birds will feast over your body!'

The two of them attempted in vain to confront each other but the swaying ranks pulled them apart. Hector again shouted, 'Forward, Trojans! Stand by me! To the ships!'

His cry was echoed by a deafening roar emitted by a thousand men. Once more the Trojans attack met with a brave resistance put up by the Greeks who answered with their own cry of war.

Hector urges the Trojans to aim for the Greek ships

45

BOOK XIV

However slow, however difficult the Trojans' progress was towards the ships, Hector's cries reached the tent where old Nestor, sitting by the wounded Machaon, awaited news of the battle's latest developments.

'Unfortunately,' he whispered, 'Hector's cries are all too clear. I shall not remain in this tent. I shall take up my post!'

The old man felt that his time had come. He armed himself from head to toe and set off to combat but he was to die in battle, crowning his long life with glory. On his way he met some of the Greek princes who had gathered on the seashore. They were all worn out or wounded.

'Ah, Nestor!' Agamemnon said. 'Hector's threats have proved true! We are defeated and our ships shall be destroyed!'

'Yes,' replied the old man, 'the wall on which we had rested all our hopes has fallen, and it will not be up to us – I so old and you so wounded – to reverse the fortunes of the battle.'

'However,' suggested Agamemnon, 'we can launch the ships to sea and so avoid them from being destroyed by the Trojans. We could sail offshore, wait for nightfall and ...'

Odysseus interrupted him, 'Agamemnon, what cowardly words you speak! You who have the honour of leading the Greeks, you speak of taking flight? After nine years of battle and sacrifices you suggest putting our ships back to sea? Don't you understand that if they see a sailing ship, none of our warriors will want to get on it? They will think they have been betrayed. They will throw down their arms. It would be disastrous!'

'I agree, Odysseus!' replied Agamemnon. 'Speak then. What do you suggest we do?'

Diomedes intervened 'Listen to me,' he said forcefully, 'we are really wasting too much time, we are wounded, it is true, and we cannot fight. Nevertheless we can stand among the fighters and urge them with our presence and voice. We can lead back to battle our scattered soldiers. Let us not linger therefore! Let's go where there is fighting!'

Fearing a Greek defeat, Nestor decides to go and fight

Thereupon the princes returned to what could have been the last battle had not Hera, protectress of the Greeks, kept a close watch over them. She did not want the triumph of Troy through the deaths of Agamemnon, Nestor, Odysseus and Diomedes.

'Zeus could be back any moment now,' she thought, 'to take the battle in hand, and there would then be no hope left. I must therefore distract his attention. I must act so that he doesn't see or think . . .'

The beautiful goddess then flew over the high peaks of Mount Ida where Zeus had taken his seat again. Before she joined the father of all gods, she called on Sleep, brother of Death. 'Sleep,' she said, 'friend and master of all, listen to me. I have a favour to ask of you. Grant me my wish and you will receive a golden chair as a gift. Make Zeus, whom I am about to visit, sink into a deep sleep.'

'I cannot unless he asks me himself. I fear his anger.'

'Sleep, if you think a golden throne is not sufficient, I promise you shall marry one of the young Graces, the sweet Pasitheë with whom you are in love.' At these words Sleep smiled. 'If you give me Pasitheë whom I love, then, O Hera, I shall make Zeus sleep for as long as you wish!'

And so it happened. Followed by the invisible Sleep, Hera pleasantly conversed with Zeus, cajoling and caressing him, while Sleep cast his spell. Slowly Zeus fell asleep. As soon as Sleep saw the father of gods asleep, he fled to Poseidon. 'Now' he announced, 'you are free to help the Greeks, O Poseidon, king of the sea!'

Granting Hera's request, Sleep lulls Zeus into a deep sleep

Aias picks a large rock and flings it on Hector who falls unconscious

Poseidon did not hesitate. 'Warriors of Greece!' he shouted as he appeared to them, 'Are we to leave victory to Hector? No! Take courage! Let us unite our efforts and form an iron wall that the Trojans will not be able to overcome! Forward!'

Revived, the Greeks tightened their ranks and marched on slowly towards the Trojans, uttering loud shouts and raising a din of weapons. Neither the wind blowing through the leaves of the great oaks, not the roaring fires in the mountain ravines, nor the sea crashing on the reef were as loud as the clamour raised by the two opposing armies.

Hector saw all the enemy princes draw nearer – even the wounded ones – but he didn't lose heart at the sight. He wielded his spear and aimed it at Aias. The blow would have killed Aias had it not hit the heavy leather belt which held his shield and sword. As Hector, still facing the enemy, withdrew amongst his men, Aias picked up one of the many boulders that had been used to prop the ships and hurled it at him. The boulder stuck Hector on the head and he collapsed unconscious to the ground.

With a cry of triumph, the Greeks lunged forward hoping to capture their hated enemy. But already the Trojan warriors were shielding Hector. They had all rushed to his rescue: Aeneas, Polydamas, Agenor, Glaucus, Sarpedon, all the Trojan princes. While a close-linked rank held firm against the Greeks' lunge, Hector was dragged back, carried into a chariot and driven to the shore of the River Xanthus. There he was revived by cold water being poured over his head. He came to, opened his eyes, looked around him, then suddenly vomited blood and lost consciousness again.

Meanwhile, the Greeks were attacking with renewed zeal. This was the opportunity they had been waiting for, the moment which might decide the fate of the day. Before Hector recovered they must hurry and strike the enemy a hard blow.

For a while, even without Hector, the Trojans held on, but many perished, others fell back, the front line yielded and soon the retreat turned to flight. Chased by the Greeks, the Trojans lost all the ground they had conquered at such a high price. They were driven further and further back until they were compelled to clamber over to the other side of the wall!

The infuriated Zeus turns to Hera who has tricked him

BOOK XV

By now, the Trojans were on the brink of defeat, but suddenly Zeus awoke from his deep sleep. From the heights of Mount Ida, he turned his gaze towards the plain of Troy and saw the attacking Greeks led by the enraged Poseidon. He saw Hector lying unconscious on the bank of the River Xanthus and immediately understood. He turned to Hera who sat by him waiting anxiously, and glared at her with flashing eyes.

'Ah! So this is what you were up to!' he thundered. 'You have tricked me, you had me put to sleep! Beware Hera,' he went on, swollen with divine fury, 'you know what my wrath is like! Remember when I hung you by your feet and left you dangling from the clouds! I can do it again!'

Pale and tembling Hera answered, 'I never prompted Poseidon to go against the Trojans, believe me, Zeus. If you wish me to, I shall run down to him at once and tell him to leave the field...'

'No! I shall not send you,' replied Zeus, 'instead you will fetch Iris and Apollo – they will carry out my orders. I have promised Thetis,' he went on more calmly, 'to do justice to her son Achilles whom Agamemnon has offended. And I shall. The Greeks shall be brought to the brink of defeat and then realize that without Achilles' help they can achieve nothing. When they reach this conclusion, Achilles will take up his arms again ... Ah, then I shall let Troy fall and Hector die. Until then,' he concluded, 'let no one dare

Iris goes to Poseidon and orders him to withdraw

stay there!' Poseidon was livid with anger and humiliation, but he could not disobey. Reluctant and cursing he went back to the sea and was immersed by the waves. Meanwhile, Zeus addressed Apollo, 'Go down to the banks of the River Xanthus. There you will find Hector unconscious. Give him back his strength and stay by his side. Help him in battle!'

Apollo swept down from Mount Ida and in a flash appeared before Hector. He had not yet recovered, he was still stunned and out of breath, but had managed to sit up on a stone.

'What are you doing here Hector?' asked the god. 'You have been hit I know. For a while you feared lest you should die, I know that too. But you won't. I am Apollo and I have been sent by Zeus to tell you to take your post and start after the Greeks again. Stand up! Go and fight! Remember I shall be by your side!'

The Trojans counter-attack the Greeks taking them by surprise

intervene to help the Greeks! And now Hera, off with you!'

As quick as lightning Hera flew to Olympus where the gods, seeing her arrive pale and distraught, gathered round her.

'Zeus is much angered,' she told them, 'let none of us dare stand in his way! Oh, it is terrible, terrible! Iris,' she added turning to the young divine messenger, you must run to Poseidon at once and tell him that Zeus commands him to leave the battlefield immediately and not to return there again. Apollo go at once to Zeus who wants to send you on a mission! Quickly do as I say! I am telling you, Zeus is beside himself with anger.'

Soon after, Iris flew to Poseidon who, trident in hand, was still inciting the Greeks to battle.

'Poseidon,' she said, 'I bring you an order from Zeus. Leave here, return to your sea and

50

Upon hearing these words, Hector felt all his strength returning to him. He felt his muscles flex and his blood rush through his veins. He stood up, grasped his spear, he picked up his shield, mounted his chariot and joined the bewildered troops.

'Follow me!' he bellowed. 'Back to the assault brave Trojans! We must reach the wretched ships and set them on fire! Follow me!' As one, the Trojans followed, facing the enemy again. And again the fortunes of the long battle turned. The Greeks who thought they had already won, saw Hector fall upon them. Aghast and frightened, they faltered, dismantled the ranks and fled. The first one to recover his courage was Thoas who shouted, 'Hector is not dead, Zeus is on his side, but let us gather princes of Greece! Let us cover our army's retreat so as to enable them to form new ranks in defence of the ships!'

At this call, the strongest fighters rushed to form a barrier which held back the Trojans for a while. Behind them, in the meantime, the main body of the forces fled in a panic towards the sea! Against Thoas and his men, several Trojan assaults failed, but it was the Greeks who were dying in ever increasing numbers.

'Never mind the dead!' Hector shouted to his companions who stopped to strip the corpses. 'Leave their armours and shields! We shall have time to collect them after the victory. Everyone to the ships now, and take the blazing torches with you. Victory is ours!'

Like a river bursting its banks and flooding the plain uncontrollably, so the Trojans moved seaward, gathering in close formation around the ships where the Greeks had retreated in a last effort to defend them. Heedless of the arrows and spears raining on him, Hector tried to set fire to the first ship. From the high stern, however, the Greeks protected the ship with the strength of desperation.

'Now is the time to die or save ourselves!' shouted Aias, trying to infuse courage into his men. To which Hector replied 'Bring the fire! Zeus is with us. When we have destroyed these ships, Troy will be saved!'

Heedless of the spears and arrows, Hector tries to set fire to a Greek ship

BOOK XVI

While the fighting continued Patroclus burst into his lord Achilles' tent. Turmoil, shouts, screams and moans could be heard close by. Yet here in the Myrmidon camp there was perfect order and a strange, eerie silence. In his tent, Achilles dressed in a simple tunic, sat quietly, as though the war he had so bravely fought in for nine years no longer concerned him. But seeing Patroclus so distraught, pale and drenched in perspiration, Achilles' face became sombre.

'What is the matter with you Patroclus?' he asked. 'You look as though you've been crying. You are crying! Why? Do you bring news of a friend's death? Or do you weep,' he added, 'because the Trojans are setting fire to the ships?'

'Yes, noble Achilles, my Lord! That is the cause! Too many are dead and wounded! If you returned to battle ...'

'No,' interrupted Achilles. 'No, Patroclus. I have been too deeply offended to fight again for Agamemnon.'

'Then,' implored the youth, 'at least allow me to fight, lend me your armour, your helmet and let me lead the Myrmidons into the field. The Trojans will think I am Achilles coming to assist the Greeks, and perhaps will not dare press their attack!'

Achilles hesitated then said, 'So be it! If that is your wish Patroclus, take my soldiers and fight. Yes,' he added, 'by saving our ships we are saving our way home. Yes, bring me glory so that Agamemnon will realize his error and will give me back Briseis. But,' he went on, looking sternly at his young friend, 'hear my advice. As soon as you have repelled the Trojans from the ships, return to our quarters. Beware of letting yourself being carried away by your longing for victory, do not follow the enemy! You must not,' he insisted, 'take from me, the honour of entering the city of Troy. And more importantly, I don't want you to take risks. Drive back the enemy, Patroclus and then let the Trojans fight on their own. Get ready now,' he concluded rising to his feet, 'I shall assemble my men.'

Patroclus could not suppress a cry of joy and he began to put on the splendid armour, which even on its own was sufficient to deter any enemy. Meanwhile Achilles prepared his Myrmidons for battle.

'I shall not be the one to lead you to the enemy,' he shouted, 'but by following Patroclus, you shall be following me! Let each of you fight with all his might!'

The eager men leapt off Achilles' fifty ships. At that moment Patroclus came out of the tent wearing the dazzling armour and cheers of enthusiasm welcomed him. He jumped into his battle chariot driven by the charioteer Antomedon and to which were harnassed the formidable horses – Balius and Xanthus. And off he set to battle.

Achilles watched him leave, and then returning to his tent he took out from a richly inlaid chest, a cup, from which no other man but he had ever drunk. After cleaning it, he filled it up with wine.

'I drink to you, Almighty Zeus!' he said solemnly. 'I am sending my friend Patroclus to battle. Give him strength, let everyone see that he can fight on his own, let him drive back the Trojans from the ships and let him return safe and sound to my camp.'

With these words, he slowly drank and emptied the cup. And Zeus heard his prayer. Of these two wishes he granted the first, but not the second. Patroclus was indeed to repel the Trojans but he was not to return to Achilles' tent.

Patroclus' and the Myrmidons' arrival infused courage into the Greeks and at the same time appalled the Trojans who thought they were facing the invincible Achilles. They drew back, then abandoned a ship to which they had finally set fire. Fighting continued amongst the ships but under the pressure from Patroclus and his warriors, there was nothing Hector could do but to call back his troops and flee.

Many were the Trojans who challenged Patroclus for they had realized that he was not

Achilles. One by one, the young warrior struck them down. Even the stalwart Sarpedon, King of the Lycians, fell, his heart pierced by a spear. It seemed that Patroclus was just as strong as Achilles and that nobody could stand in his way. Then Hector drove straight at him in his chariot, steered by Cebriones the charioteer. Patroclus waited, a spear in one hand, a stone in the other. At the opportune moment he threw the stone with all his strength which hit Cebriones full on the forehead. He rolled in the dust, while the chariot, no longer steered, veered dangerously. In readiness, Hector had jumped off the chariot

just in time to push back Patroclus who had pounced on the charioteer's body.

The fierce duel between the two warriors soon became a ferocious battle. Around Cebriones' corpse fell a hail of arrows and the Trojans and the Greeks fought fiercely. Swept by the ardour of the battle, Patroclus forgot Achilles' advice to retire directly after the enemy had been driven back from the ships. The ships were by now far behind and Troy was getting closer and closer. There Patroclus ventured, slaying furiously at everything in his way. There he was destined to find death.

Patroclus flings a stone at Hector's charioteer

54

BOOK XVII

During the violent fight over Cebriones' body, Achilles' young friend was in fact stabbed in the back by a spear thrown by Euphorbus. His armour came undone and his helmet – Achilles' pride – rolled in the dust. The wound was not mortal but Patroclus felt that he could no longer fight. Staggering and losing blood he dragged himself back amongst the Myrmidons. But Hector saw him and did not hesitate. He lunged at him with a spear and stabbed him below the belt. Without uttering a sound Patroclus fell to the ground.

'You thought you would take Troy, Patroclus!' Hector exclaimed triumphant. 'Instead I have killed you! This is the end of the road for you! You will not enter my city but you shall serve as a meal to the vultures!'

'That's right, Hector,' replied Patroclus with a failing voice, 'boast about my death. You have not long to live. Achilles himself will avenge me. You shall perish by his hand ...'

'Who knows?' retorted Hector, 'Perhaps Achilles is to die before me?' But Patroclus could no longer hear him; he was dead. Hector then stripped him of his armour and put it on himself, and on his head he placed the helmet that belonged to Achilles, his greatest rival.

Watching Hector's vainglorious act, Zeus muttered, 'Ah, unfortunate warrior! You wear the arms of someone who is feared by all and you cannot feel that death is close upon you! No, your wife Andromache will not see Achilles' armour and helmet. I shall not allow you to bring them back to her as trophies. But in exchange for death which is soon coming to you Hector, I want to give you a great victory today!'

Hector puts on Achilles' armour after stripping it off Patroclus

*Greeks and Trojans fight over Patroclus' body in a
ferocious battle*

And once again Hector felt driven forward.
Wielding his spear he renewed his assaults on the
enemy. They fought furiously over Patroclus'
body. The Greeks would not tolerate to see it
taken to Troy and thrown to the dogs. The
Trojans, on their part, could not lose such a
testimony of their triumph.

Taking the first stand in defending the blood-
drenched body was Menelaus, who stabbed the
young Euphorbus to death. Then Menelaus was
joined by the awesome giant Telamonian Aias.
Together they held back the first Trojan onslaught on their own. Gradually more warriors
came to their rescue and Patroclus' body was
fought over mercilessly. On the one hand, holding him by his head and arms, the Greeks tried to
pull him to safety towards the sea. On the other,
tugging at his feet, the Trojans attempted to drag
the corpse into Troy. Streams of blood gushed
everywhere.

Amongst the swaying ranks of the medley
whose intensity never abated, Hector and Aias
looked for each other, never succeeding in
coming face to face. It was almost impossible to
tell whether it was day or night or even whether
the sun or the moon shone above them. Over the
battlefield hung a blanket of dust under which
the opponents clashed, struck, fell, killed,
wounded or died. It was to be a day of intolerable
exhaustion, a day of stifling heat, a day without
pause in which many would die.

'Greeks! We cannot return to our ships with-

out Patroclus' body!' someone shouted. 'We would rather the earth swallowed us alive!'

'Trojans!' came the answering cry. 'Even if you are all killed beside the corpse, let none of us retreat!'

Far from the conflict, Achilles' horses, Balius and Xanthus, had come to a halt and standing motionless they wept. Indeed, hot tears were streaming down their eyes, and dropped to the dusty ground. The animals mourned their Patroclus who had so often steered and driven them. Seeing their grief, Zeus himself was moved.

'No!' he said troubled, 'No, I promised you that Hector would never drive you! Take heart and do not be afraid to cross the battlefield in order to carry the loyal charioteer Automedon back to the safety of the camp to rest.'

Escaping the reins of the ailing Automedon, the two neighing steeds galloped off and entered the battle at full speed making their way through the bewildered fighters. They pressed across the battlefield like a terrible vision and finally reached the seashore.

The day was drawing to its end and the fate of Patroclus' body was still uncertain.

'One of us,' shouted Menelaus 'must go to Achilles with the news of his friend's death. Perhaps when he finds out he will come himself to save his friend's body! Antilochus,' he went on, turning to a companion 'the sad duty falls to you. Go to Achilles and tell him that Patroclus is dead!'

BOOK XVIII

Meanwhile, in his tent, Achilles was overcome by a dark premonition. His heart told him something terrible had happened. He stepped out of his tent and stood motionless listening to the rumbling of the battle ... It was growing nearer, as at first it had grown further ... The Trojans were therefore advancing again.

'Perhaps this means that Patroclus has been wounded or is dead?' thought Achilles. 'But how could it be possible? Did I not tell him not to press on towards Troy?'

At that moment Antilochus appeared: 'Achilles, an unforeseen misfortune has befallen us. Patroclus is dead. Hector has killed him and stripped him of his armour and they are fighting over his body.'

On hearing the news, Achilles was thunderstruck. For a second darkness dropped over his eyes, for a second he was drained of his blood. Then he let out a howl of grief to the sky and fell to the ground in great convulsions as though he had lost his mind. He poured ash over his head, tore at his hair with his own hands under the eyes of his appalled friends and slaves. Then he rose and held Antilochus' hand, who was weeping uncontrollably. Achilles ran to the sea. From the depths of the sea his mother Thetis heard his cries. At once, gliding over the waves, she reached the shore and came to him, 'What is it, dear child,' she asked. 'Perhaps the Trojans have not retreated from the ships they wanted to set alight? Perhaps ...'

'They did withdraw, Mother. But Patroclus is dead,' replied Achilles. 'I have lost him, I have lost my weapons. I have sent to death the friend whom I loved better than myself and now I can do nothing for him. Help me, Mother, help me to go back to battle and may my destiny take its course.'

Sadly Thetis said, 'Yes my son. I shall be back at dawn to bring you new weapons. I shall ask Hephaestus to forge them for you. Wait for me. Then you can go back to battle and may your destiny take its course!' With these words, Thetis vanished.

Thetis appears to Achilles and promises the help he seeks

*Achilles weeps over Patroclus' body and swears to
avenge his death*

In the meantime the Trojans had launched a new attack, determined this time to get hold of Patroclus' corpse at all cost.

Achilles had started to weep again, when in a dazzling light appeared Iris, the messenger goddess.

'Patroclus' body is about to be lost and you, Achilles, you weep and do nothing!'

The hero muttered, 'Hera has sent you Iris, and you reproach me. But how can I go to battle when I have no weapons?'

'You need no weapons. Come out of your tent and show yourself at the trench where the Greeks are being driven back by Hector. Let them hear your voice. That will be enough. This is what Hera has to tell you.'

So Achilles left his tent. An aura of fire seemed to shine around his head. With long strides he moved toward the trench beyond which the battle raged. Taking a firm stand he let out a howl of grief, rage and threat ... The Trojans heard him and, perplexed, they came to a halt. Achilles cried again. The Trojans dared not press on, their princes held the horses back, looking round anxiously. Is Achilles returning to combat? No. But for the third time Achilles howled and suddenly the Trojans were panic-striken. They fled and never stopped running until they had taken refuge inside the city! So ended the day which could have brought them a decisive victory. The Greeks therefore retrieved Patroclus' body and carried it to Achilles' tent. Embracing it, Achilles wept.

'Patroclus,' he said, 'I promised to bring you home alive and covered in glory. I did not keep this promise, but I shall keep another one: before I join you in the kingdom of the dead, I shall kill Hector!'

Throughout the night wailing and lamentations rose from the distraught Greek camp.

Hephaestus forges new armour for Achilles

Meanwhile, Thetis had gone to Hephaestus, the blacksmith god, and had found him among his puffing bellows, hard at work, beating the anvil with his mighty hammer. As he saw her, Hephaestus rejoiced and limped over to Thetis. He had never forgotten how she had hidden him and given him shelter in the sea when, as a child, he had run away from home, where his mother – ashamed to have a crippled son – would have him locked up. 'Ask me whatever you wish, Thetis,' he said joyfully. If I can do it, I shall. Perhaps it is already done.'

Thetis told him about Achilles' sad story and concluded, 'So Hephaestus I have come to ask you to forge a helmet, a shield, leggings and armour for my son. He no longer has any of those for Hector, the murderer, has stripped them from his beloved Patroclus.'

'You shall have what you ask for,' replied Hephaestus and at once he set to work in his smoke-filled workshop. First he made the shield: huge, sturdy with a triple rim, and he engraved it with the symbols of the earth, the sea and constellations of the heavens, also with pictures of cities, temples and rural labour scenes. Then he started on the armour and forged one brighter than the blazing fire. He shaped a tall shining helmet to fit perfectly on Achilles' head. And on top of it he placed a golden crest trailing a long horse's tail. As for the leggings, he used tin so that they would be light to wear and would not hinder his running. Never had a mortal seen more beautiful or stronger weapons. When Hephaestus had at last finished, he handed the arms to Thetis who swept down like a falcon from Mount Olympus, to take them to her son.

60

BOOK XIX

Achilles was still weeping over Patroclus' body when Thetis arrived with her shimmering load. 'My son,' she said 'stop crying! Here are the weapons you have asked for. Hephaestus has forged them for you. Put them on and let your destiny take its course.'

At the sight of the weapons, the Myrmidons around Achilles whispered in utter wonder, so great was the impression of might given by the armour, helmet and shield. Achilles carefully surveyed the gifts from his mother and Hephaestus, and said, 'Before I wear these to battle, it is necessary that I reconcile myself with Agamemnon. I am already paying too bitterly for the anger caused by the offence. I pray you divine mother, save Patroclus' body from decay!'

'I will, my child. But do not linger, do your duty.'

Achilles went to the seafront and with a thunderous voice called for the Greek troops to assemble. Hearing his voice and his words, the Greeks trembled with anticipation and hurried on to the centre of the camp. There in front of all the princes, many of whom were wounded, Achilles walked towards Agamemnon with outstretched arms in a sign of peace and solemnly declared that he renounced any thought of anger and revenge.

'I can see,' he said, 'that our feud has only proved beneficial to Hector. But let us now forget the past. Let bygones be bygones, Agamemnon. We must only think of fighting. Come lead your army to battle, I shall be at your side.'

Achilles walks to Agamemnon with outstretched arms in a sign of peace

The beautiful Briseis is taken back to Achilles' tent

Moved, Agamemnon replied, 'Greeks, friends, I should like to say that when I offended the noble Achilles, I was not myself. I know I was wrong but, believe me, it was not I who spoke, it was not I who offended. It was as though a demon had taken possession of me. No, Achilles, I am not responsible for the outrage I have caused you. What has been has been, you are right, but I want to make amends even for a wrong that was not of my doing. You shall receive from me all the gifts you want, and with them you shall receive my friendship!'

'The gifts can wait,' exclaimed Achilles, 'let us turn our thoughts to battle. Let us go now!'

Odysseus, who had been wounded during the fight, rose to speak, 'No Achilles, we cannot go to battle now. You come with us and victory shall not escape us. But, my friend, we are still too worn by the tough struggle we have just sustained. Only a few of us and our warriors have had a chance to eat, and you mighty Achilles, are well aware that strength depends on nourishment. Let us first take some food then we shall resume our fight with renewed energy.'

Achilles listened impatiently to these wise and prudent words. He wanted to avenge Patroclus at once. But everyone agreed with Odysseus. Before he prepared for battle, Agamemnon sent Achilles the most precious gifts: seven tripods, twelve mettlesome horses, twenty splendid copper vases, ten gold talents and seven young slaves all talented at domestic work. Then solemnly and according to Greek tradition they carried out the sacrifices for the consecration of peace and reconciliation. Finally, the young and beautiful Briseis, who had been the cause of the fatal anger, was taken back to Achilles' tent. When the young girl saw Patroclus' corpse she knelt by it and began to wail, scratching her cheeks and breasts in despair.

'Alas, my very dearest Patroclus,' she moaned, 'I shall never be able to speak to you again, we shall never again make plans for the future. I have found you but never as I thought I would: dead, you are dead!' They all wept and Achilles looked on somberly. And he remembered the time when they had spoken of war together.

'Patroclus, I shall die under the walls of Troy,' Achilles would often say, 'such is my destiny: a brief but glorious life. But you Patroclus, you will go back to Greece and you will relate my exploits ...'

Odysseus and the other princes urged Achilles to take food. Weakness could overcome him in battle and betray him. But the youth stubbornly refused to eat or drink! From the peaks of Olympus, Zeus then turned to Athene, 'Just like a child, Achilles does not want to eat. Still he must not be left to starve. Run my daughter and distil into his breast some nectar and ambrosia – divine food – so that he will not be robbed of his strength in the middle of the battle.'

Athene promptly obeyed and suddenly Achilles felt his usual strength return to him. He stood up wiping away the last tears. It was no time to weep but to fight. The Greek warriors sitting between the ships and the wall so bitterly fought over earlier, had now eaten and prepared for battle. Achilles gave orders for the Myrmidons to be ready to move on, then he started to dress. With eyes blazing like fire and gnashing teeth he slipped on the armour forged by Hephaestus, fastened his sword belt, secured the shield on his arm and, finally, placed on his head the helmet adorned with the shimmering horse tail. He then entered his tent and took from a case a formidable spear, so long and heavy that he was the only one among the Greeks who was able to handle it.

When he reappeared he was greeted by roaring cheers from the whole army, Automedon then drew up in the battle chariot to which Xanthus and Balius were harnassed, both pawing the ground impatiently. Achilles leapt onto the carriage and with a deep voice said, 'Xanthus, Balius, when the fighting is done, bring me back alive! Don't leave me there dying on the field as you left Patroclus!'

Through a miracle performed by Hera, Xanthus answered, 'Yes Achilles, we shall save you. But remember the hour of your death is drawing near. And on that hour we can be of no help even if we run like the wind. It is your destiny, Achilles to be defeated in battle by a man and god!'

Stamping his foot impatiently the hero replied, 'Xanthus, why do you speak of death? I know that I must die here, far from home! But before this happens, I will have avenged Patroclus and defeated the Trojans. Let's go now!'

With that he gave the cry of war and ordered his charioteers to set off. So leading the Greeks forward, the city of Troy appeared in the distance, tightly enclosed within its walls.

Achilles puts on the new armour forged for him by Hephaestus

BOOK XX

The battle between Greeks and Trojans was about to start again. And up above on the peaks of Olympus Zeus called all the gods to a solemn assembly. He insisted that all be present. With great sternness he said, 'This is a decisive time in the war. I shall not move from here but you may intervene in the battle according to each of your likes and dislikes!'

At these words the gods immediately flew down to the plain which stretched between the city and the sea. Athene, Poseidon, Hephaestus and Hera sided with the Greeks. Aphrodite, Ares, Apollo and Artemis with the Trojans. As soon as the immortals touched down on the battlefield, the fight began furiously.

Flying into a temper amongst the clashing troops, Achilles on his chariot, searched for Hector in order to challenge him. Ares noticed it

and came up to Aeneas, 'Aeneas, Achilles is approaching. Go to him, stop him, kill him! You will reap eternal glory and you will save Troy!'

Aeneas knew he was not as strong as Achilles. He had already fought him once, yet he did not hesitate. He stepped forward and upon seeing him Achilles shouted, 'Why do you come to me, Aeneas? Do you think you can defeat me and so be rewarded by Priam with the crown of Troy? No, listen to me. Go back now, unless you want to die!'

'Your chatter will not make me run Achilles!' replied Aeneas, and he launched his spear which for all its speed and power was not able to pierce Achilles' shield – the work of a god. The young Greek, in his turn sent his spear whistling through the air and it pierced Aeneas' shield like a bolt of lightning. The bronze-headed spear

Achilles and Aeneas fight each other in a duel and Poseidon protects Aeneas

missed Aeneas by a hair's breath and sank into the ground beside him. Achilles unsheathed his sword, Aeneas picked up a rock and brandishing it over his head was just about to throw it. The duel would certainly have ended with the death of one or the other hero if Poseidon had not intervened.

'No,' he whispered, 'I do not want Aeneas to die. A great destiny is reserved for him – that of perpetrating the Trojan race through the centuries!' And he flew ahead and sprayed a dense mist around Achilles whose vision became blurred. Poseidon then pulled the spear from the ground, laid it at Achilles' feet and swept Aeneas off, propelling him to the very back of the Trojan ranks.

'Do not fight with Achilles again,' he warned, 'but know that when he is dead and gone, no other Greek shall ever defeat you!' Having spoken these words, Poseidon returned to where Achilles was and lifted the mist. The hero saw his spear lying at his feet, but no Aeneas.

'This is indeed a miracle,' he muttered. 'Anyhow, I knew that Aeneas is loved by the gods . . . Well, never mind,' he exclaimed, and picking up his spear he called to his men, 'there are other Trojans to kill! Friends, follow me, I cannot deal with them alone and fight for you all! Let each one of you confront his opponent and slay him as I shall do!'

For his part, Hector was encouraging the Trojans, who at the sight of Achilles were already faltering.

'You must not be afraid of this man!' he shouted, 'They have taken Troy with words but they never will in reality! Were he made of fire, I

65

would still challenge Achilles!' His men answered him with a cry of war and the din of the battle.

Achilles was achieving wonders killing, one after another, numerous Trojan heroes. When the very young Polydorus, Hector's brother, fell, Hector was overcome with grief and sought instant revenge. Making his way among the fighters, he sought to challenge his rival in a duel. Achilles shouted, 'Come Hector! Come and meet your end!'

'Don't try to frighten me!' replied Hector and he cast his lance. He would not have missed had not Athene, as quick as lightning, warded it off, saving Achilles in the nick of time. Achilles then prepared to strike but it was Apollo's turn to intervene. He hid Hector in a dense cloud where Achilles threw his spear four times, in vain.

Hector throws his spear at Achilles but Athene diverts it and saves him

'Ah, so you escape me, you cur!' he exclaimed. 'A god has saved you again, but I'll have done with you. Do you hear me, Hector? Sooner or later I'll have done with you!'

He returned to his chariot and whipping the horses, Automedon the charioteer plunged into the thick of the battle. Like a fire blown by a gale destroying dry forests, so Achilles swept the enemy ranks, mowed down Trojans who stood in his way and trampled the wounded men, in his uncontrollable fury. The chariot's wheels, the axle and the hooves of Xanthus and Balius were spattered with blood, and also covered in blood advanced the invincible Achilles.

BOOK XXI

The Trojans withdrew in panic. The disorder turned into irreparable chaos when they reached the Scamander river. Terrified, they fell into the water, seeking salvation on the opposite bank, hoping that Achilles' chariot would not be able to cope with the current. But Achilles leapt from the chariot and taking only his sword, he chased after the fugitives across the water and slaughtered them. Nobody dared to stand up against him, nobody dared to turn round and face him. Finding no resistance, the hero killed without respite, without mercy, not even for those who, unarmed and wounded surrendered and begged to be spared! Soon the river became tinged with the dark colour of blood, soon horrendous islands of corpses surged to the surface. Helmets, shields, armours cluttered the banks and amongst the dead floated the spears. In the water the implacable Achilles continued to strike.

At the sight of so much blood and such ferocity, the god who lived in the depths of the Scamander river swelled its waters and crashed them against Achilles. The waves lashed and choked him, blinding him, overwhelming him in an attempt to knock him down and crush him against the sand and mud. Weighed down by his armour, Achilles struggled desperately and realized that he had reached the limits of his strength.

'Is it then to be so,' he moaned. 'Am I to drown like an imbecile?'

The god of the Scamander river swells its waters crashing them against Achilles

Ares and Athene quarrel and engage in an open battle

Indeed that would have been his end had not Hephaestus rushed to save him by assaulting the river with his flames and compelling it, after a hard struggle, to calm its waters and cease harassing the hero.

The fight between the Scamander river and the lame god triggered off a brief but heated feud between all of the gods. From the start of the Trojan war they had been divided. More than once they had disagreed and Zeus had had to threaten them so that they would not come to blows with each other, but now the time seemed to have come. Ares threw himself into the battle where Athene was already fighting furiously against the Trojans.

'Why are you here? Once you guided Diomedes' spear to wound me. Well now it is my turn!' And with this he struck a formidable blow on his sister's helmet. But the helmet could even withstand Zeus' thunderbolt and Ares' blow came to nothing. The goddess retorted at once by hurling a boulder which reached its target. Ares was hit in the neck. He groped blindly trying to keep his balance but his breath had been taken away and he stumbled onto his knees.

'You silly fool!' said Athene mockingly. 'You want to fight with me and you don't even know I am stronger than you!'

The lovely Aphrodite then rushed to Ares' help. She took him by the hand helped him to his feet and led him away from the field. The outraged Athene chased after her and knocked her down!

'Ha!' she exclaimed before her battered rivals, 'If we immortals had fought, the war would have been over long ago and Troy would no longer be standing!'

Meanwhile Poseidon had challenged Apollo but the latter had replied that he did not wish to fight. The haughty Artemis reproached him harshly, urging him to take up the challenge. But Hera flew to confront her.

She plucked the bow off Artemis' shoulder and beat her until she took refuge by Zeus' feet, in tears. It was to there, around their father, that all the gods finally returned when they had done with fighting. Some in triumph, some humbled, some vexed. But all the immortals maintained that the Greeks had shown more courage and determination.

Among the gods back at Olympus, Apollo was still missing. He had gone back to Troy, determined to defend it with his presence.

Inside the city old Priam climbed up the tower and watched the battle anxiously. When he saw his warriors withdraw in disorder, chased and slaughtered by Achilles, he ordered, 'Open the gates! Let our men find shelter in the city! But be careful to shut them in time, beware not to let Achilles in!'

His command was obeyed but how would the fleeing Trojans enter the city. They were by now trampling over each other, they would be crushed in the rush to cross the threshold. They would perhaps be slaughtered to the last! Apollo was well aware of it and so left Troy to try and avoid the catastrophe. He flew to Agenor, the valiant warrior, and inspired him with courage, calm and determination. Agenor who was running with the others, stopped at once.

'Why am I running?' he thought. 'Why do I let myself be driven by the others? I am not afraid of Achilles! He is a man like the rest of us and like the rest of us he can be killed. I shall not run but instead I shall face him!'

He turned around, wielding his spear, 'Achil-les,' he shouted, 'do not think that you are going to sack Troy today. We are not all frightened of you!' And he launched his spear which struck Achilles under the knee, and had it not hit the leggng made by Hephaestus, it would certainly have broken Achilles' leg. In his turn, the unscathed Achilles prepared to attack. But Apollo intervened and surrounding Agenor with a mist, swept him off to safe ground. So that the Trojans could pass through the open gates, the god took on Agenor's appearance and appeared in front of the confused Achilles.

'So you are still here then!' the hero exclaimed, and brandishing his bloodstained spear, he threw himself in hot pursuit of the man he thought was Agenor and who was running desperately across the plain.

'I'll catch you up, coward!' shouted Achilles at his heels, and overcome as he was with rage and craze for revenge, he could not have imagined that the fugitive was not Agenor but Apollo in disguise. Neither did he realize that he was being led in the opposite direction of Troy. So the exhausted Trojans, no longer hounded by Achilles, were able to enter the city, close the gates and allow themselves at last, a little rest.

Achilles chases after Agenor on the plain not knowing that it is Apollo in disguise

*Hector sees Achilles advancing and waits for him,
spear in hand*

BOOK XXII

However, not all Trojans were able to enter the safety of the city. One of them remained outside the walls: Hector. There he stood alone in front of the Scaean gate, spear in hand, waiting.

Meanwhile Apollo had stopped running. He cast off Agenor's appearance and resumed his own. Then mockingly he turned to Achilles and said, 'Why are you chasing after me? Can't you see I am a god and that you cannot kill me because I am immortal?'

'A god indeed, the most disastrous of all!' replied Achilles angrily when he realized he had been made a fool of. 'If only I could kill you Apollo, I would take my revenge on you!' Then he spun round and dashed back towards Troy. From the tower, Priam saw him running back.

'Hector, my son,' he shouted, 'come inside the city! Take shelter, do not stand up to Achilles! Save yourself and with you save Troy!'

Hecuba, the hero's mother also begged and moaned and held out her arms in desperation. But Hector gave no answer. Yes, he had also seen Achilles approaching, he also felt that the supreme moment was close but he did not wish to go inside the city. He did not want to flee and mar his honour. He could have ordered his troops to retreat earlier, as soon as he had seen Achilles join the battle, but he had not done so and he would now pay for it. What was to be done? . . . Throw down his arms, surrender and return Helen back to the Greeks? . . . Hector knew full well that in any case Achilles would not grant him a moment's truce, that he would not accept his surrender, that he would not have mercy on him. Better to face him then, and at last one would know which one of them Olympus wanted to cover in glory!

A weighty silence fell on the entire plain and Hector and Achilles came face to face. Something quite unexpected then occurred. Hector, whose courage until then had been unswerving, was suddenly panic-stricken. Seeing his great rival advance on him, gigantic and menacing, surrounded by a magic aura of light as though the sun glowed through his bronze armour, Hector's heart faltered.

He was unable to look at the vision, he was unable to stand his ground. He turned his back on Achilles and fled. Yes, he fled, heedless of the Trojans who watched from the wall or the

Greeks who had drawn closer in silence. He fled and circled the walls of Troy three times with Achilles at his heels.

Meanwhile, at Olympus, Zeus had been weighing Achilles and Hector's lives on his scales and saw that it was Hector's time to die.

'So be it!' he murmured solemnly.

That is when Athene played the last trick. Speeding down to Troy, she assumed the appearance of Deiphobus, Priam's son and caught up with Hector in full flight.

'Brother!' she cried. 'Stop! Don't wear yourself out so! Let us both confront Achilles, come!'

Out of breath Hector replied, 'Yes, Deiphobus, you are right. Enough of running! Achilles!' he shouted turning round, 'It is you and I now! Let us fight, but let the victor return the body of the defeated!'

Achilles draws his sword and runs towards Hector

71

Achilles answered, 'No I shall make no pact with you! You are as good as dead, Hector! You shall pay for what you have done to Patroclus!' He had barely finished his sentence, when Achilles launched his spear. Hector was ready for it and leapt aside and the lance sank into the ground.

'You have missed Achilles,' exclaimed Hector the Trojan, 'my turn now!' And he thrust his spear but it bounced off the shield made by Hephaestus.

Hector turned round, stretching his right arm: 'Deiphobus!' he cried, 'give me your spear . . .' He stopped short – there was no one about him. He understood and muttered, 'Ha! the gods are indeed calling me to death! This is one of Athene's tricks. Well I shall not die without glory!' He drew his sword and lunged at Achilles . . . but the latter had already raised his own spear which the invisible Athene had picked up and put back into his hand. Taken by surprise, Hector could do nothing to defend himself. He was struck in the neck by the deadly weapon and collapsed to the ground.

'You thought you would remain unpunished, Hector!' exclaimed Achilles, 'Now the dogs will have your body!'

'Achilles,' implored the dying Hector, 'by all that is sacred to you, I beseech you to return my body to Troy . . .' Then death took him.

While Troy resounded with cries of lament, the triumphant Greeks rushed forward, gathered round the fallen hero and savagely thrust their spears into his corpse!

'Ha!' they shouted, 'He is softer now than he was in battle!' Then Achilles tied Hector's feet to his chariot and howling, lashed his horses into a gallop. Dragging his rival's corpse in the dust, tearing it apart and defiling it, he drove round the walls of Troy before going back to his camp.

Achilles ties Hector's body to his chariot and drags it in the dust round the walls of Troy

BOOK XXIII

All the Greeks had by now rejoined their camp, removed their armour and put down their arms, at last thinking of resting. But Achilles ordered the Myrmidons to remain armed. 'Come with me!' he added. 'We must pay our respects to Patroclus, we shall rest afterwards!'

His orders were obeyed and together with his warriors, he wept on the seashore, calling out the name of his friend.

'I have kept my promise, Patroclus,' he sobbed. 'I have killed Hector and I have thrown his body to the dogs'.

The wailing rising from Troy was echoed by the weeping rising from the sea. Even after the Myrmidons had finally taken off helmet and armour, even after they had fallen to the ground in utter exhaustion, Achilles continued to lament, alone, on the vast beach.

The following day a huge pyre was prepared on which they put the embalmed body of Patroclus. Solemn sacrifices were carried out, then Achilles set fire to it.

'Be happy in the Kingdom of the Dead, Patroclus! You have been avenged!' In total silence, the Greeks watched the flames consume the young hero's body whose ashes were gathered and placed in a golden urn which was buried by the sea.

In the meantime, something strange had occurred. Not one dog had approached Hector's body which had been thrown in a corner. Apollo and Aphrodite had taken care of the poor mortal remains and protected it from further laceration.

Patroclus' funeral was over. But Achilles raised his hand and in the solemn silence he shouted, 'Friends, wait! Before you return to

The winner of the boxing match will be given an untamed mule and the runner-up a beautiful cup

trained in domestic work. The contenders were the gigantic Telamonian Aias and the shrewd Odysseus. The latter was shorter and not as strong as his opponent, but no less skilled. Grappling they both fought for a long time and neither one was able to bring the other down. The wrestling match dragged on and the spectators were getting bored.

'Let's do this,' said Aias, 'the first one to lift the other off the ground will be the winner. Agreed?'

'Agreed,' replied Odysseus. The first attempt was by Aias. He would easily lift his rival off the ground and he was about to do just that when Odysseus kicked him on the shin. Taken by surprise, Aias dropped to the ground. There was general bewilderment. Such a big man had yielded under Odysseus's weight? It was now Odysseus's turn, but as hard as he tried he could not lift his giant opponent. Achilles then intervened, 'You have both won and shall receive equal prizes!'

The winner of the wrestling contest will receive a tripod and the runner-up a beautiful slave well skilled in domestic work

your tents, I ask you to honour one more time my beloved friend. In memory of him, I want you, valiant warriors, to measure your strength against one another. In the name of Patroclus I want you to compete in a contest of skill and power. I shall draw the prizes from the treasures of my war booty.'

And so a boxing match was suggested. The winner would be given an untamed mule and the runner-up a splendid cup. The noble Epeius stepped forward and challenged everyone by saying in a loud voice, 'Whoever wants to fight me can step out. But let your friends stand by to give you a hand when I'll have finished with you!'

Epeius was not boasting! After a brief fight, he knocked down, with a terrific punch, the only man who had accepted the challenge, Euryalus. He was carried unconscious and covered in blood to his tent. Achilles then suggested a wrestling match offering a huge tripod as first prize and for the loser a beautiful slave, well

The games continued with a spear-throwing competition. At first the champions competed in a sort of duel: whoever succeeded in scratching his opponent's skin and draw a little blood would be the winner. The challenge was between Diomedes and Telamonian Aias. They confronted each other with great zeal but neither succeeded in wounding the other. The game then became dangerous. Indeed the contenders' fighting spirit was frightening and the concerned spectators called for the competition to be suspended and that both be given equal prizes.

More spear-throwing challenges followed. Agamemnon and Meriones presented themselves. Before the two of them could measure their skill, Achiles said, 'Agamemnon, every one knows that no one can surpass you in spear-throwing. Then take this copper vase and to you, Meriones, I give a sturdy lance!' All approved and with this gesture peace amongst the Greeks was sealed and the memory of the feud erased. Thus ended the games in honour of Patroclus.

An embossed silver dish will be awarded to the winner of the foot race. A fat ox will go to the runner-up and half a gold talent to the third contender

Diomedes and Telamonian Aias compete in a spear-throwing competion

A foot race then took place for which the first prize would be an embossed silver dish. The runner-up would be given a well-fattened ox and the third contender half a gold talent. Moving forward there was Aias, son of Oïleus, followed by the young Antilochus, son of Nestor. And to everyone's surprise there came Odysseus, tired as he was from his struggle with Aias. From a line marked out by Achilles the three champions set off running. At once Aias took the lead distancing himself from Antilochus but he could not succeed in outrunning Odysseus who kept close behind. The spectators standing cheered as the two opponents covered the last stretch.

'Help me to win, Athene!' prayed Odysseus and the goddess came to his aid, making Aias trip and roll on the ground just as he was about to cross the finishing line. One stride and Odysseus won the race.

'You were helped by a goddess,' grumbled Aias. But Antilochus said, 'Well, I admit, young as I am, I can do nothing against old Odysseus!' And they all laughed heartily.

*Priam kneels before Achilles imploring him to return
his son's body*

BOOK XXIV

Several days went by without any fighting whatsoever. Achilles' grief did not abate. Every morning after spending the night wandering and sighing on the seashore, he tied Hector's corpse to his chariot and dragged it three times around Patroclus' tomb. The corpse of the dead hero did not decay, however, as Apollo had taken pity and protected it!

But he was not the only one to pity Hector. The other gods also begged Zeus to put an end to the horrendous butchering on the one side and to Priam's sorrow on the other. Zeus sternly agreed. He sent Thetis to her son to persuade him to return to Priam his rival's body, and he sent his messenger Iris to Priam to urge him to go trustingly to the Myrmidons' camp. Hermes would lead him.

So with his chariot loaded with precious gifts for the ransom and some linen sheets to wrap his son's body, the old king left the city at night and, led by Hermes stole unseen into the Greek camp. He reached Achilles' tent where he was sitting

sadly with some of his most loyal friends. Priam then stepped out of the shadow and knelt before Achilles.

'Achilles,' he said, 'think of your Father! Take pity on my grief! Give me back my son! Look,' he added, 'here I kiss the hand that killed him!' And he took Achilles' hand and kissed it. Achilles was astounded to see the old king in his tent. Moreover he was moved by his words and his behaviour.

There was no more anger nor rancour in his heart, but only sorrow and compassion. He whispered, 'Ah! Old man, I can see how much you have suffered! But how could you find the strength to come to my tent alone. You know you have put yourself in mortal danger by coming here. Certainly some god must have helped you. Weep no more Priam. You have no cause for it. Yes you have not come to me in vain, and nor in vain will you have reminded me of my Father. He too, like you, is destined to suffer because my fate is to die under the walls of your

Troy. Don't cry old man, do not grieve any longer!'

After shedding a few tears, the hero raised Priam to his feet. He then ordered his maid servants to wash Hector's body, perfume it and to wrap it in the linens brought by the King of Troy. Going back inside the tent, Achilles said, 'Take your son. Enough tears for now. Come, eat and drink with me, in honour of Hector.'

Whereupon the young hero and the old king both sat at the table facing each other and in great respect of each other. Achilles was strong and brave. Priam was wise and prudent. They were both of equal nobility. At last, Achilles asked, 'How many days will you devote to your son's funeral?'

'We shall mourn him for nine days and on the tenth we shall bury him. On the eleventh we shall have a feast in his honour, then we shall be ready to fight again,' answered Priam.

'Then for twelve days I shall suspend all hostility,' said Achilles in a low voice, and as a sign of loyalty he pressed the old king's hand.

Soon after, Priam sadly mounted the chariot where his son's body had been placed and in the great silence of the night he returned to Troy.

From the top of the tower, his daughter Cassandra recognized him as he approached and shouted, 'Trojans! Come out and see! Hector is returning to his homeland! Come and see!'

They all hastened and the city's gates were opened wide to let in the king's chariot and its sad burden. Hector's body was laid in the centre of a room in the palace. Amid the weeping, the wailing and the lament arrived the beautiful Andromache. She knelt, looked at her husband's livid face and whispered, 'You have died too young Hector, and left me too soon. And with me you have left our son. He cannot yet talk, but Hector, I fear he will never live through his youth now that you are no longer here to defend him.' Andromache wept. By her side old Hecuba and the beautiful Helen wept, and throughout the palace and throughout the town the vast crowd wept.

But Priam ordered, 'Enough now! Bring fire wood for the pyre and you can gather it outside the walls without fear for Achilles has promised to suspend the war for twelve days.'

For nine long days, while the wailing continued, they gathered firewood from the surrounding countryside. They built a gigantic pyre on which Hector's body was finally placed. Then they set it alight. When the last ember of the pyre was put out with wine, the hero's ashes were gathered into a golden urn which, wrapped in purple cloth, was then placed inside a tomb and covered with huge stones. Then, according to

Priam returns to Troy with his son's corpse

Andromache weeps over her husband's body

custom, all assembled in Priam's palace and sat at the funeral banquet.

These were the last honours rendered to Hector, the Horse-Tamer.

Hector's death did not mark the end of the war which was yet to last, and it was not even to end with Achilles death – shot by an arrow from Paris' unerring bow. The destiny of the hero who had chosen a brief but glorious life had followed its course. But Troy still resisted.

Troy was to fall by deceit. It was to fall when the Greeks, accepting Odysseus' advice, pretended they were lifting the siege, and on the seafront where their camp had stood they left a gigantic wooden horse. In that horse (which the Trojans mistook for a divine gift) were hidden the most stalwart Greek warriors. In the still of night they came out of their hiding place and this time there was to be no salvation for the city. The gates were opened and the Greeks sailing back to shore under the cover of darkness, marched into the city inexorably. Massacres and fires marked the end of Troy. Almost all its defenders were killed, Hector's young son was killed, old Priam was killed. But their memory was to last forever like the memory of their victors.

Achilles would be eternally celebrated, and eternally honoured as would be his unfortunate rival Hector who was killed in defence of his homeland and his people.

The Trojans lead the wooden horse inside the city walls, thinking it is a sign from the gods